C000269279

I, City

PAVEL BRYCZ

I, CITY

translated from the Czech by
Joshua Cohen & Markéta Hofmeisterová

TWISTED SPOON PRESS

PRAGUE

Copyright © 1998 by Pavel Brycz
English translation and afterword © 2006 by Joshua Cohen, Markéta Hofmeisterová
Copyright © 2006 by Twisted Spoon Press
Author photograph © Karel Cudlin

All rights reserved under International and Pan-American
Copyright Conventions. This book, or parts thereof, may not be used or
reproduced in any form, except in the context of reviews, without
written permission from the publisher.

ISBN-10: 80-86264-27-0
ISBN-13: 978-80-86264-27-1

This translation was made possible by a grant from
the Ministry of Culture of the Czech Republic.

contents

an appearance, heroic

If you stop at the corner of two streets — there among
the small houses you might know as Na Špačkárně, in
the quarter of the city irreversibly called Stalingradská
(at least that's what people still call it, for there is no
greater paradox of history than calling the small by
great names) — you will encounter two memorials to
the victims of the miners' strikes of Most.
The strikes numbered two, during them eight people
were shot. One strike was in 1920, the second and
more famous one in the Year of Our Lord 1932. I am
not a poet, I am a city, ill equipped to write about the
affairs of people. I am a city, a new city. I cannot bear
witness to the past, I can describe only what I see.
And here, among the full-grown, needle-leaved shrubs,
I see a stone.
And on the stone:

THIS & THAT, FROM HERE & THERE, AGE, MINER
THIS & THAT, FROM HERE & THERE, AGE,
MASTER SHOEMAKER

One sunny day in June, a twenty-six-year-old poet
born in Old Most brought his friend Pedro from
Lisbon to the memorial.

The poet thought he'd introduce his friend, the
Portuguese poet, to the utter absurdity he experienced
in his every encounter with the memorial to the
miners' strikes. He laughed at the mere memory of the
Youth League shirts worn by he and his Gymnasium
classmates, released from afternoon lessons and
obliged to stand astride the officers of the army and
the people's militia. Comrades laid wreaths, another
comrade delivered a speech, and after the address the
Internationale was sung. The Gymnasium boys, like our
poet, were born in the year 1968. They couldn't stand
memorials, comrades, Youth League shirts or wreaths.
And they couldn't stand the *Internationale*.
But they liked playing pranks.
"So we also sang the *Internationale*, to the grumbling
of those fat old farts, who were in uniform, with their
rifles slung over their shoulders, but we sang it in the
original, in French," Most's poet explained to his
Portuguese friend. "They were totally confused, as
were our teachers, and the army officers as well, none
of those comrades knew what to do, even given their
excellent cadre profiles, the lessons they'd learned
about crisis development engraved deep in their faces.
They didn't know whether they were supposed to
forbid our singing as an impertinent provocation, or
to appreciate that for the first time we were singing
along with them, in unison.

"We sang, and in so doing we laughed at their parades, at their memorials, at their eternal fear of a freedom that for them was only the recognition of necessity."

Most's poet finished his story, and approached the memorials. The Portuguese poet read to himself the names of the long dead as well.
And, suddenly, they became completely serious, and forgot the laugh for which they had come. No longer was there the absurdity of the *Internationale* and the Youth League shirts. Only the two of them and the shot dead remained, and the young men felt a profound sadness for the fact that people sometimes don't know how to be people.

I am only a new city, not a person.
I am not a hero. I have never defended my walls. But when people on my streets and in my houses are truly human, I feel heroic.
I have remembered these poets.

an appearance, nostalgic

Sometimes, I feel like meeting my Old Town. I dream
that my new streets would hitch to its cobblestones,
that the Běla would flow through the old riverbed and
me and Old Most would be Siamese twins, the Gemini
glued, the Moon in conjunction with the Sun.
I know it's not possible, and the remnants of Old Most
only reassure me.
I'll never step into the same Běla twice with my Old
Town, but if cities die like everything else alive on this
planet, then I believe that one day we'll meet in
Paradise.
Until then, with me it's like in that poem upon the
theme of the UNENCOUNTER, which a man dedicated
to a woman he never met:

> No, I didn't see you in the Berolina neon —
> a circus that came from the Alps.
> Perhaps the huge elephants hid you from view —
> perhaps the camels, perhaps the darkness.
> You were in the front row with a beautiful lady?
> But I was there, too!
> Both of us with mommies —
> the pistachio ice cream . . .

No, I didn't see you in the whirl of masks —
perhaps my pride was evil.
Perhaps the cowboys hid you from view —
perhaps the princesses, perhaps the darkness.
You were in the mask of a beautiful lady?
But I was, too!
Both of us with mommies —
the pistachio ice cream . . .

No, I didn't see you at our school's ball —
perhaps I was drunk as a Dane.
Perhaps the white mice hid you from view —
perhaps the camels, perhaps the darkness.
You sat in the gallery with a pretty lady?
But I was there, too!
Both of us with mommies —
the pistachio ice cream . . .

What more can one say?
Sometimes, all the pistachio ice cream runs out.

an appearance, amorous

Love is a Magnetic Mountain. If it gets hold of you, it doesn't let go. It will never forsake you. I, city, know that well.

For ten years, on the sidewalk under the windows of the boarding school, I LOVE YOU had been painted in red by an unknown author, until — with the rain, snow, and sun — it was gone.

All the girls living behind those windows could confirm this. Speaking for them all, there is, for example, Zora Vesecká — child star of '70s television — who, during her short stay in the city, observed herself as the object of this declaration, too.

I remember the inscription of an unknown vandal on the wall of the army barracks:

MY GOD, MY GOD, WHY HAST THOU FORSAKEN ME?!

Who so desolated his heart?

And who was the author? Was he a soldier, a student of theology, or possibly both?

Both.

He who has not been to Hněvín has not been to Most. And what citizen hasn't been there on a date at least once in his life?

Well, as I've said:

Love is a mountain.

Hněvín is a Mountain Magnetic.

an appearance, linguistic

Prague is a small Paris. Whenever you come to the Champs Elysées, you can meet Prague there. She is small, lost, crying, she takes you by the hand and wants home.

Most is also Prague, Paris, Babylon, but linguistically speaking. As people came to metropolises from all over the place, a tangle of languages arose. It's not any different in Most.

After all, nearly all Mosters have made their ways here from other places, and by now their language has become an industrial conglomerate. From the older residents you can still hear the influence of hard Sudeten German. And so the Czech of my citizens doesn't sing like the speech of Hradecers, Budějovicers, Brnoers or Břeclavers.

Hearing the talk of a Moster, you can most often mistake him for a Praguer.

Yet it is possible to sing even in the Czech of Most. It is, however, a song of a burnt tongue, of a burnt land, and so all the more convincing.

Everyone who cares for it has a soul, though short of breath from the everlasting smog and distressed by the great expanses of concrete apartment blocks — yet a soul. And only a soul gives words meaning and joy to speech.

Believe me: though I am only a city, I don't want my heart's people to be mute.

I want to be their lost child on the boulevard of the Champs Elysées, who they take under their wing and lead home.

an appearance, wintry

They were cold; they trudged through the mud with nowhere to go. So they went to the planetarium to look at the stars. They wanted to lie alongside one another, to look at the stars up above them; they wanted to get warm. But in the planetarium, the dazzling sky tore free, all the stars went off to the movies and he and she stood helpless in the lobby of the House of Culture. They were fifteen and didn't know what to do next.

Then they had the idea to peek into a hall that was giving out an odd old music.

It was Ellington, performed by The Original Prague Syncopated Orchestra with Ondřej Havelka. The concert hall was packed. Laura and Her Tigers (all of them) and Most's miners' brass band were there, too.

The usherette seated Him in the only free seat on the left side of the hall and Her on the side opposite. Ondřej Havelka was singing an Ellington blues:

> *Yesterday I fell asleep real bad,*
> *and had myself this dark dream.*
> *I was in New Orleans,*
> *and I was a slave*

with great white teeth
to ground great anger down.
Great white bales of cotton,
O I'm soaked to my soul.

Clouds laze above the plantation.
I'm just a scarecrow in a field.
I dream about warmth and a bed.

But my old bed,
it's back in Africa.
Here in New Orleans,
with no white elephants.
I don't give a good goddamn.

Maybe I would've woken up
from this dream, but it was slavish.
It didn't set me free,
I'm deep in it forever.

Lucky for me, instead of elephants
New Orleans trumpeted jazz to me.
And I recalled.
My African soul.
Far from Kilimanjaro.
But close to the heavens.

He and she. They completely forgot to hold hands.

an appearance, poetic

Once upon a time there was a café called the Poesie. A nice story is related to it. Maybe it's a legend; maybe as time went by many things were fabled onto the facts. I don't know.

One thing is certain — in the time of the Poesie Café a group of young men who wanted to be *poètes maudits* would meet there. They initiated themselves into the guild of the accursed poets with the drinking of wine spritzers, the use of coarse expressions, and the reading of Villon, Baudelaire, and Rimbaud.

Among much else, they were adamantly convinced of their early death, their genius, and that they would be misunderstood by their contemporaries. They were seventeen, they were five, and they would never have admitted to themselves that they were actually the boys from that novel by Karel Poláček.

They felt an affinity with the darkest chords of the human soul. They were enticed by Sigmund Freud, interpretations of dreams, and suicide. They were able to talk for the longest hours about these three subjects. Every now and then they wrote something as well. As opposed to the profundity of their discourse, their verses were as shallow as a split of champagne.

Then one day our poets decided to write a collective

work, which would serve as their manifesto, and in which they would reach the absolute depths of their lyrical capabilities.

It was, for them, a temptation as tremendous as bungee jumping from atop the highest bridge.

And this was the result of their efforts, a poem into which they poured everything that a seventeen-year-old can feel and write if he has four friends, sits at the Poesie Café, and drinks watered wine:

THE BALLAD OF THE ETERNAL MOTHER
AND THE UNGRATEFUL CHILD

I thank You that You gave birth to me,
And I would thank You more,
If from Your clutches You set me free,
Mother Murderess, O let me soar!
Here I cry, mourn deep in Your womb's lair,
Anxiety the altar of my waking muses,
To enter the World and not just anywhere,
In which self-love a suicide seduces.

I met a girl, a woman, a Savior,
Beauty and needful, wants a lord to smother,
My body going mad, my soul for her favor,
From the waist down, nothing but mother!
My mouth to a girl! My heart and another!

My eyes to a girl! My breast, hers!
But clenched by my own mother,
My man's might boxed in a hearse!

No other dreams now and now why,
At night alone I am dreaming,
Of You, the star in my sky:
In the earth my desire wants for burying,
In Your desolation there is mine —
Loneliness where there are no ruses,
You beside me and entwined —
My self-love a suicide seduces.

Five mothers then read the poem, and five mothers found they had no understanding for the poetry of their sons. One evening, after the closing hour of the Poesie, the poets had nowhere to go, as their fathers had disinherited them, then banished the disinherited from their homes. They spent a gloomy night at the train station. The trains were running and then they stopped; the loudspeaker sounded oppressive silence; it was night and there was nothing left to do other than to be deserted and sad, and so they were deserted, sad, and accursed. Luckily, their mothers and fathers soon came to their senses and the poets didn't have to live at the train station any longer; they could graduate with peace of mind and seek life's fulfillment.

And because one of the five stayed in Most, was assiduously enterprising, earned money and wisely invested, after some time he could buy even the Poesie. He fixed it up, replaced the upholstery on the seats, and rechristened it the Prince Restaurant.

Since time immemorial all seventeen-year-old suicides end in this way. It's time that kills them, and the circles made by a stone thrown on the surface of the water are to be seen only for a brief moment.

an appearance, occupied

When remembering the Russian occupation of August 1968, I think of painting. And that of painting the apartment of an ordinary family in an ordinary apartment block on my main street. Mr. Novák stands atop a stepladder, dips the brush and above the paper cap on his head lays on broad swaths of white paint. Mrs. Nováková stirs the paint for him and every now and then hands him a beer, with a pointed warning: "Karel, don't you fall down!"

And Mr. Novák first goes glug glug glug, and then claims: "True enough, though after beer I have a little difficulty with my feet on the ground, on this stepladder I don't seem to have any problem at all . . ."

And though I could continue describing the beautiful dialogue of this married couple, who bring yin and yang, the anima and animus, and so philosophy, peace, and harmony even into ordinary painting — the brother of Mr. Novák all of a sudden bursts into this idyll and roars: "Dear people, while you're painting away here without a care in the world we're being occupied!"

Mr. Novák quickly climbs down the stepladder, and indeed without it he wavers a bit after the beer, and together with his wife Mařenka and his brother Břéťa

they open the doors to the balcony to hear the same
sound they had all heard before in their strollers and as
men in the army, a sound they wished never to hear
again, especially on the main street of their city.
"Now it'll never dry!" Mr. Novák proclaims, gazing at
the tanks tearing the asphalt of the main street with
their treads, their noise tearing the eardrums of those
great pals of Mozart, those pitch-perfect Czechs, the
pennyweight heroes for whom Blaník had been
exchanged for Bílá hora.
And for ages men disappeared into pubs and boys
didn't grow up to be men, though their dreams were
of such kind as if they had long ago formed The
Brotherhood of Cremation.

an appearance, sporting

The hall opposite the boarding school with a stadium
at its side has to have some strange genius loci.
Consider the enormous amount of human sweat that
has evaporated here over these many years. That
surely gives off a substantial whiff of something. The
hall simply savors of humanness.

I, city, can smell the humanness, too, and I know
what it costs a boxer for a TKO, a table-tennis player
a winning ball, a basketball player a basket, a handball
player a point, and . . . and . . .

Simply, a sea of sweat.

And beyond this, for many boys and girls this hall
represented not only a ticket to the world of sport, but
also an invitation to the palace of art. Concerts of pop
singers and bands were held here, and it was possible
to go through the dressing room and directly into the
concert without paying admission.

Who wouldn't be enchanted by this strange world
from the other side? When coming through the artists'
entrance and you sense the crowd as a rhythmic quiver,
the entire expanse of the sporting hall is for you at that
moment rhythm materialized, thrusting into you like a
small tattooing needle. You mustn't move fitfully, you
mustn't violate the rhythm; you have to be in synch

with it to keep the pained tears from your cheeks. And if you succeed? It's like an orgasm touching eternity. Though it lasts only a short while, it can reproduce you to the infinitude of being.

Then the sweat and the rhythm reverberate in the atmosphere for a long time after. And if I gaze into the sporting hall, I become all bathed in sweat.

And if I hit up against the needle wrongly — also in blood.

an appearance, may

If there is a month of May, the high-school graduates have its number. They can't play catch up on the lost months.

Not that they don't know anything, they do. Nor that they wouldn't be in love in the very month of love. That they are, too. Headfirst in love, up to the ankles. What they lack above all is a class photograph, which would be placed in a shop window to present them to the crowd on the streets. "Look, that's us — who better?" it should proclaim to the world. And it should be bold, original, and bright.

But there's none.

The boys suggested photographing their bared behinds, but the girls didn't want to enter their new lives with naked asses. Young women suggested the styles of the 1930s, replete with pageboy haircuts framing sweet impish smiles, but Cossacks in their late teens don't want to look like they just stepped out of an old-time movie. Boys wanted to be lynched, girls Barbie dolls; men suggested caricatures, women touch-ups . . .

There were a great number of suggestions, including the oddity of inserting an X-ray of a stomach or lung into the class photograph.

In the end, they didn't do anything at all.

And now they have May.

They can't play catch up on the lost time.

They gaze into the shop window with despair. We so looked forward to it.

And then nothing.

Then, graduation's behind them. They look at their new life.

They looked forward so much.

And then nothing.

And every year, it's repeated. Students gaze into an empty shop window.

Pardon me. It's not empty. Of course. It's full of refrigerators, televisions, vacuum cleaners, hi-fi stereos, bathroom fixtures, miscellaneous wall units, who knows what else.

Students dimly reflect in the shop window, as if the window didn't need them at all.

an appearance, sudekian

O, to master life left-handed. And to do so in such a
way that you remain forever immortal!
Who wouldn't wish that? I knew one of these masters.
He achieved immortality and people bow to him even
today.
He was Josef Sudek. A crazy, single-handed photographer.
Crazy and beautiful.
He came once in the sixties. He came and photo-
graphed me. My outskirts, my landscapes, my
beautifully sad forsaken ruins and the rubbish among
the hillsides that no longer exist. And I tell you, if a
city wore a hat, I would lift mine, for he mastered all
of that left-handed, and his photographs live on still.
"Most — Immortal" I would entitle those photographs, if I had the right to do that.
But because I, city, am without a hat, I can only beg
my inhabitants: Take your hats — it doesn't matter
whether they are new or old, bought or inherited —
and in the same moment, when I tell you on the wind,
lift them.

an appearance, gypsy

I'll confess something to you, my dears. I'm not a
Gadjo. Seriously not. At least not purebred. And it's
not only because I love Gypsies who straddle the
boundary between girl and woman, and it's not only
because I love horses, too, and music, when it goes to
the hips, bosom and heart, I feel like Johann Sebastian
Bach . . .
That's how it is, my dears, I'm a nomad.
Mine is a migratory soul. And one day you'll wake up,
and you will be somewhere totally different than you
are today.
You've already experienced it once. Don't you
remember?
You looked on in astonishment as the church rode away.
Where does our faith ride? In which direction is our
lack of faith headed?
To heaven or to hell, which is the destination of our
future? Shhh . . .
Once before you watched the church slowly going, and
the birds were off to the south.
You didn't know what was behind it. Now, I'll reveal it
to you: I, city, unhappily happy, hitched up invisible
horses and dreamt of a promised land. And I dream
about it still, incessantly.

Forever with you, though leaving. Think of the deacon's church, which is a bond between . . . my Christianity and my Roma longing.

an appearance, manly

When is a man born? Maybe it's when his relatives
first peek into his swaddling clothes, or when he stops
wearing those repulsive orange corduroys handed down
from his older sisters; or maybe when he dies and only
a silence remains in his stead, such a silence that everything has to be started all over again as in the beginning of the world, and God has to say all over again:
Let there be light, so be it, and then let there be water
and earth and animals and people, too, and let it all be
good, because when a man dies, the world, which
loved him, goes with him as a loyal spouse of an Indian
Maharajah, and for a moment there is nothing, and
silence?!
Yes, that's how it will be, perhaps . . .
"Let there be light," I, city, repeat after God, thinking
all the while of myself, whether or not I'll ever rise
again, after the greatest of my men has died. And I
know I will. I know I will be. Lessened only of one
man. Lightened only by his laugh. His laugh, which he
brought with him from Moravia, along with his violin,
when he came to settle the border regions after the
war. A teacher, he had been everywhere on the map of
the world he taught. And had been there a bit sadly,
forcibly assigned, and so running away and scaling the
Alps, hungry, frightened and playing in his native

Haná "Where is My Home," to laugh at the Gestapo, because he was the Last Moravian, like those from Letohrádek in other heroic times.

He remained like that to the last.

He, a man of wine and love. He defended me. As he was a Latinist, at sixty-five he without a care in the world stood up to a beer-filled horde of vandals who were giving me such a beating that the windows were falling out of my bus stops.

He, a man and the Last Moravian and violin and wine and love and Latinist and Where is My Home and against him a sieg heil of hoodlums — he pitied them, for the beating they were giving to the city and him, because there is no one with legs that are long enough to run away from himself, when he has in him spite and a small house painter named Adolf Hitler.

Still bleeding from the temple, he was thinking of his violin and protected his hands from the vandals so that he could still play the songs of his Hanka Haná, as he nicknamed his little Moravia.

No, a couple of boys couldn't hurt him, who was so much above them. Just as they couldn't hurt me.

The old man lived with the violin for a long time after. With it, he told me stories short and long, about Hanička Haná and about his life, how he had said goodbye to it a few times during the war and yet here he is still, old as Methuselah.

And then . . . one day. But what could I tell you — you

know it all already! The world died for a moment. And then it created itself anew. As our pupil František from the city of Paris would write: "He left and cannot be found."

And as Pavel Brycz, a copywriter for the EuroTel advertisement, would write: "He left and didn't take his cell phone with him."

We'll never be able to call him anymore, to tell him that though he might have become a Titan, we always loved him as he was, and that without him here we're only little lost boys, who though now without a violin still sing his song about Hanka from Moravia . . .

All the hills around the river
Today I would forget gladly
Not to think about your bosom in November
Not to think about your bosom in November.

Today in our sad cold river
We took for a mirror gladly
There is no place for the two of us anymore
There is no place for one.

And below the dam there lives the sun
And the echo under the bridge is fervent.
Hanička . . . Hana!

Shrieking, burning still.

an appearance, pigeon

He wanted to become a pigeon. Another son of the
city. He wanted to fly and to fly away, whenever he
needed to. He needed to often. When he ignited his
parents' carpet with Kanagom glue, when he lay down
on a street to hitchhike a car up to Paradise, when he
climbed a high-voltage pole, when he stood on a tram's
shaft-bar, when for the first time he fell four over the
legal limit for alcohol and wasn't able to get up again.
He needed to become a pigeon, when he was in love
and she thought he was only being dirty. He needed to
fly away, when he got a taste of "ginger," speed, and
not the kind they make in Pardubice. He needed
wings. He needed to wave to the world from high
altitude. Now he's gone. He sniffed Čikuli stain
remover and flew off far away from me, though he
lies dead on one of my streets. I, city, don't know how
to shed tears. Because of one boy, the rain won't fall
from the sky.
I know, he was mean. Neither his mother nor father
could love him.
Whoever met him avoided his mean eyes.
And now here he lies, a police photographer immortal-
ized his face, sleeping, not tired from all the fights
and all the rage in his heart. They'll send his face to be

exhibited in MEMENTO MORI. You'll see a face you won't recognize.

You'll shield your eyes in horror.

Ecce, homo!

I know, he was mean and the punishment was harsh.

But I saw him wrestling with a boa constrictor below a big-top, and only to prove that he didn't know from tears did he allow the coils of the snake to break a few of his ribs.

Do you know what he did with the money he won?

He invited those who feared him and banqueted them.

That was his nature.

If only he were a pigeon! If he only had wings!

Then he could fly away from the eyes of all and preen his wounded feathers, invisible, all the way up on the highest spire of his city.

an appearance, cosmic

"Hug me," said the boy to the girl.

"Hug me or I'll strangle you," the voice added, all of a sudden breaking into a sobbing barely suppressed.

There was darkness. The stars were not shining and the electric lamps were out of order.

I couldn't see a step in front of me, I, city, who should be aware of everything around.

Something desperate was happening here. A boy and a girl were becoming confused with one another, and were left totally in darkness. Yet a short while ago they likely sat in the twilight of the Kosmos Cinema gazing up at a love story. Yet a short while ago the stars on the screen were likely glowing for them.

"We'll always have Paris," Humphrey Bogart said to Ingrid Bergman, "We'd lost it. But we got it back last night."

Doubtless these two also dreamt that they would always have something.

"Your soul wouldn't mind being pleasured by an émigré in a grand hotel. What's worse is all this darkness suddenly around us," says the boy.

I, city, am listening to their desperate voices and there is nothing I can do. I can't move. I can't run away when love is on its way out.

I have to wait, wait patiently until another day.
After the sunrise, to see only two bronze figures,
statues outside the cinema, held in an eternal embrace.
As if nothing had happened that night.
As if love hadn't left?
Perhaps those two fell from Mars!
Or was it they who were whispering during the night?

an appearance, christmas

He stopped for the girl on the way from Prague.
It took him a long time to persuade her to get in, that
he wouldn't hurt her. She'd been leaving a bloody trail
behind her as she walked the road from Prague on
high heels. He saw she was a small runaway.
In her palm, she held a small secret. The driver looked
straight ahead. He didn't want to frighten her. To
drown the silence of her fear and clenched knees he
turned on some music. It was a foreign song. The girl
recognized the singer was singing in Spanish, or
Portuguese.
"Are you water, or only a thirst on my way?" the driver
translated.
"Oh," said the girl.
They didn't talk anymore.
He dropped her off at a crossing before a department
store. He was afraid to wish her Merry and Happy
aloud, and so he wished it to her in his heart. He saw
what the girl needed most was some rest.
To take off those bloody pumps of hers.
He was driving away and turned off the music; he
wanted to think.
Is the world really only a shelter for those forsaken?
The girl was thinking, too, as she stood at her parents'

door. Is there still time, or is it already too late for everything?

Is there silence or accusations between her mother and father? What's happened with them since she left? Have they grown old? Have they grown old like she has? They'd been beautiful, she remembered them as they were. She took after them both, the most beautiful girl in Most.

I, city, should know that.

Now she's not anymore. In three years, you can change beyond recognition. And you can get ugly when you live in a manner that turns your stomach.

And hers turned often. Once, she even vomited on a Salvador Dalí painting.

It was in Prague in 1988, in the Sternberg Palace at the exhibition of the Guggenheim collection.

Back then Dalí wrote her:

"Thank you. Since Gala died, there's been no woman really able to give me a rise."

By then the painter already lay on his deathbed and wished very much for something to rouse him.

But memories of bulimia brought the girl images much more horrific than those of Dalí. In pain, she whimpered like a cat seven times whipped when a certain man cured her with his fists so that she wouldn't lose her figure for the customers. She closed her eyes. In her palm, she still clenched her secret. She couldn't leave; she had to ring at her parents'. It was Christmas Eve, and she needed a bit of love.

They opened: and they hadn't grown older by even a hair.

Rather, they'd grown younger for this very moment. It was Christmas Eve, after all. Their daughter had been gone and now she'd come back. And her father wasn't at all as severe as she remembered him from her childhood. And her mother was silent and attentive.

Is this my family? Have I rung at the house of strangers? Aren't I asleep?

Really, she was very tired. She wanted to sleep and was glad her parents didn't ask questions.

After so many years, she slept alone in her bed, having pulled off her pumps full of blood.

She was sleeping and her father and mother saw how her harsh expression melted away.

"Look, Mother, it's our old little girl again," whispered her father. "She's not old, don't you see, she's growing younger right in front of our eyes!" her mother laughed.

And then the girl inadvertently let loose her fist and something fell from it and rolled on the floor. The father bent down and picked the thing up. It was mace. Father, Mother and I, city, stared at the canister of tear gas and we knew then that our daughter had definitely returned.

And that now she won't make anyone cry.

an appearance, donkey

As long as I've known him, that little donkey's been an ass.

He loved cigarettes and grubbed them; everyone gave them to him.

He was a small donkey.

Maybe he wasn't so stupid after all.

Maybe he was wiser than the Marlboro Man, the man from the ad.

Fact is, everyone wants to ride on horseback, and so thousands of children from Most have gone to, still go, and will always go to the horses kept at Svinčice.

And as long as that small donkey Ferda was around, he ate all their cigarettes. The children couldn't light up so often, like the Marlboro Man on the horse. They could only every so often run away from the little donkey, make a small fire and light up the last cigarette they'd saved. And just from that one cigarette they got so sick that they told themselves, smacking their foreheads, "only a donkey could like this." Next time, they gave him all their cigarettes. And so the little donkey was making a simpleton of himself solely for the sake of the children's health, and only the tobacco concerns the world over would call him an ass.

He was a fox, that little old donkey!

an appearance, innocent

I knew a grandfather who didn't want his grandson to get in with any bad company. He's never gotten into any company at all. When he made love, he made love alone; on tennis courts he bounced a ball against a wall without end. When he grew up, he drank alone, and died totally alone, too.

It wasn't his fault. The easiest thing in this modern world is not to fall in with any company whatsoever. Though his grandfather didn't know this. He lived and died in other times. He was a gardener, a volunteer fireman, philatelist, chess-player, and God knows what else. He knew the modern world only from pamphlets: "How to Save Your Grandson from Bad Company." And I, city, who have never been a judge, today I will at least be the advocate of these boys when the world judges them. Forget the pamphlets, Pops!

These stupid pamphlets are named "How to Die Totally Alone" — I hope they've become outdated once and for all.

an appearance, sinful

Sinful people are not only to be found in the city of
Prague — believe me, we have enough of them here.
For example, take Mr. Hřebejk: he never put on pants
for a walk in the park.
Though he'd been a soldier. With iron discipline.
Every morning he got up at six. And exercised.
In the park he performed the Parade-Marsch,
executing turns as on a field day.
He looked good, a veteran from Buzuluk — if he had
at least worn his underwear. How Mrs. Hřebejková
tried to talk to him! But he never took a hint, just
marched and marched, and only because he was shot in
the head in that stupid war.
Or what about Mrs. Nováčková, that shameless slattern
of a woman? She brought men into the apartment, so
her husband dragged himself through the streets with
his eyes fixed to the ground, as if hypnotizing the
earth's crust to swell up and swallow him, and didn't
reply to the salutes of his acquaintances, because he
was ashamed, and at work at first he whispered until
he fell totally silent, and in his building he got onto
the elevator on principle from the cellar so that he
wouldn't have to meet fellow tenants on the ground
floor — the man was that ashamed.

He was so ashamed that he would get lost not only in the cellar, but further underground. He would die of shame like old man Bovary, if something hadn't suddenly happened. Waiting in front of the door to his apartment, in which his shameless wife had a visitor, he heard a desperate cry come from within and out ran his wife's lover. In the bedroom, Mr. Nováček found Mrs. Nováčková with a knife in her heart.

Mr. Nováček spent six years in Bory prison.

It's true that he served for another man, but no less than Sigmund Freud, the expert on the psyche, would tell you that a man taken among men as an avenger of infidelity is in their eyes still a man, and not a non-entity waiting for the elevator in the cellar or a doormat to be walked all over by the woman he loves. And so you see, dear, it's not only Prague that has its Dalibor. Mr. Nováček regained his voice and self-assurance. He advised those without sin how to cope with the sins of a sinful people.

But since people without sin don't exist, he advised all. From time to time you can see him in the Park at the End of the Line, trotting alongside the marching Mr. Hřebejk. Two cracked old men on a walk.

an appearance, fairy-tale

I knew one old lady. She lived on Skupova Street. Her
hair was silver and complexion pale.
And eyes black, mysterious as her walks.
Where would she emerge from a walk, you never knew.
In which place, in which century.
Her name was Eva Ezechielová.
Where did she have relatives? In Auschwitz. And in
Israel.
Her relatives were there, but she lived here alone. Old
and forgotten. From century to century, she took long
walks.
She talked to herself. She fed pigeons, sparrows and
tits, though it was foolish. Everything living she fed.
And with old fairy tales she fed her memories.
I wouldn't feed on memories of such kind; I'd let them
rot. I'm a city and have to remember all, but memories
of such kind I wouldn't feed, I'd kill them all . . .
And yet a man understands better than I do that he has
only one life, though it is lived between Auschwitz and
Israel, and that he has to learn to love it.
Such was her walking fate, such were her fairy tales. To
write them down, she could have done that, she could
have been famous; but she didn't write them down, and
only the sparrows and other living beings, which she

fed, and the city, which she fed with her presence, still remember them. Once upon a time. And it would have been better if it hadn't even been once . . . One freezing December day in 1942 a son was born to Auschwitz camp commandant Klaus Schön. It was all right to have a blonde wife, to be fair-haired and to be a commandant at Auschwitz. It was all right to bring into the world a child that would be fair-haired and would one day command the masses. Klaus Schön could have been content.

Not even the Führer himself has what I have — he caught himself in the heretical thought and was glad that the Magi at the Leader's headquarters didn't yet know how to read minds.

He approached his wife and child. It's a big day today. Tonight I'll drink champagne, he thought. He undid his son's swaddling clothes, and how great was his disenchantment!

His Aryan boy had an imperfection of the last boy in any village. His wonder son had a defect, foreskin constriction, medically known as phimosis. Scheisse. Incredible. Secret. Top secret! His father roared to the heavens.

At that time another man had his turn. A *mohel*. A circumcist. Only he could perform a circumcision on the boy, only he could see him — as he would take the secret to his grave.

"Lord, you saw my misery and you turn your face again to me," the *mohel* Moshe prayed to his God without benefit of phylacteries. Then, he performed the circumcision under the strictest of hygienic conditions, in absolute isolation and with submission to God's will.

For the *brit milah*, the "covenant of circumcision," he didn't have the luxury of the ten righteous men representing the delegation of Israel, he didn't have anything with which to fulfill with dignity the covenant of Abraham.

Nevertheless, the prophet Elijah came and stood by his side to assist him, and nevertheless the wonder-rabbis from Prague, Galicia, Lublin and Bilgoray visited him, too. Also the Golem was there, today nearly human.

He heard a great voice.

Tears of joy entered his eyes. God spoke through the mouth of Abraham:

"As for you, you shall keep my covenant, you and your descendants after you throughout their generations. This is my covenant, which you shall honor, between Me and you and your descendants after you: Every male among you shall be circumcised. You shall be circumcised in the flesh of your foreskins, and it shall be a sign of the covenant between Me and you. He that is eight days old among you shall be circumcised; every male throughout your generations, whether born in your house, or bought with your money from any foreigner who is not of your offspring, both he that is born in your house and he that is bought with your money shall be circumcised. So shall My covenant be in your flesh an everlasting covenant."

Abraham finished his speech. Elijah flew high up to the heavens. The *mohel* Moshe kept his promise, and followed them. When the Russians liberated the camp, they were very much surprised to find the camp's commandant clinging to a small black-haired Jewish boy more than to his own life.

So ends this fairy tale about human pride.

It was the God of Israel Who through the circumcision chose the boy's fate.

The meek lady on a walk.

Through Skupova Street, bowing to the sparrows, pigeons and stray cats — such is the way she bows to life.

Shalom, Mrs. Ezechielová.

Good day.

an appearance, hollywood

I've always loved that Hollywood gold dust, flying
from the embrasure of the film projector's booth to
the screen of the cinema. How many times have I
bent a head backward, like boys throwing crumpled
tickets and chewing gum wrappers into this dust to
see them flare for only a moment? How many times!
No wonder that today, too, indeed, right this slow
second, I sit in the movie theater watching the end of a
film entitled *Winnetou: Last of the Renegades*. And while
Winnetou and his white brother Old Shatterhand are
disappearing toward freedom in the bluish range of the
Rocky Mountains, the usherettes rise, rattling their
rings of keys, making it all too clear that the death
knell of the Rocky Mountain dream had just rung.
A handful of spectators, who for the past two hours
had dreamt of freedom, with discipline relinquish that
freedom and leave in a rush, as if running from their
very shadows, which steal across the wall and always
only across the wall, shadows nailed to the bodies as
some dark outer skeleton.
Is it all over?
Wait up! What's going on? I, city, to whom no
restriction of walls applies, because I myself am walls,
and no restriction of space, for I myself am space — I

continue sitting and see that I am accompanied in the row by a man gazing at the credits of the ending film as if through them he himself wanted to get all the way to Canada and maybe even further, as if in them he read some cipher, some message that he had to decode until the usherettes draw the curtains; and yet he has to go on decoding it, even as the usherettes turn off the lights in the theater, still, even though the lights in the lobby of the Mir Cinema flicker as they fade, incessantly, even when the key rattles in the lock from the outside after the usherettes have all left.

Good night, ladies! I think, and with amusement I watch the young man — he's about thirty years old — whom they've locked in here.

Only now does the man realize where he is, and he runs out of the theater. He hurries through the empty hallway to the door, seizes the handle, gives it a couple of jerks back and forth.

But only for a moment. Only for appearances.

He doesn't kick the locked door. He doesn't swear. He doesn't gnash his teeth, doesn't throw his body against the door. He only smiles a bit.

He doesn't break out in maniacal laughter.

He doesn't slap his thighs, doesn't chuckle so that the cinema's vaulted ceiling would fall.

He only smiles, scarcely to be seen in the dark. Then he thinks.

Not that he would think as others would think, or even think at all. Rather, he dreams.

A man with a head so thoroughly deranged by a movie starring Pierre Brice and Lex Barker, he's nearly crazed. A man locked into the Mir Cinema by the usherettes. What a headline for the tabloids!

A skillful scribbler would write:

HE STOLE THE CINEMA ALL FOR HIMSELF.

"A man, 30, for unknown reasons spent the night in the Mir Cinema. Mental state of said person is subject to examination by a specialist. Particulars about this unusual case will be made known in the next issue."

Though I am a city, I'm not interested in the tabloids. I'm interested in a story. And what really happened to the man who would become the hero of this story, whose supporting characters are a cinema, the night, usherettes, *Winnetou: Last of the Renegades* and who knows what else. Perhaps the man isn't the only hero of this story. Not by a long shot. Might his father be no less a hero?

Isn't that possible?!

What if the man, who remained alone in the cinema, had visited a cinema for the first time with his father? What if he was eight and they were showing *Winnetou*? What if there were no tickets left? And what if his father then talked an usherette into letting them in on the stairs and what if this usherette had let a whole hundred of fathers with their sons into the sold-out *Winnetou* and all of them had to stand next to the seats, stood during the movie as one stands for the anthem and stared enraptured at Winnetou and Old Shatterhand, as the two men made themselves brothers through blood — ah, how the father Karl May had to be so very happy and lonely when he first wrote them — and they, father and son, have never stood together in the cinema since; they've sat, but never again together, even though they, too, had been fraternized through blood.

And what if they never get another chance?

Because in this world men and women part all the time. This can be sadly seen in *Winnetou*. I, city, know that well.

They don't stand here anymore, a hundred fathers and sons, as one stands for the anthem, and the usherette, who let herself be talked into it, is nowhere to be found either.

Only this strange man is here, the hero of a story without a plot, and so how can he push the story along to a resolution? I'm keeping my eye on him. He's just decided to show himself, once again, the film with Pierre Brice and Lex Barker. He goes and pries open the door to the projection booth.

"How does this machine work?" he thinks looking at the projector. He feels he's pried open the door for nothing. He's forced his way into a place where he doesn't know what to do next; a million other stories about men and women come to mind. How many times have they conquered themselves with love, and then they don't know what to do next.

He sits with his head deep in his palms and thinks. He has a friend who served in the army as a projectionist; he'll call him to come, not realizing that it's a strange request, certainly crazy, illogical and altogether impractical, because for the sake of this request he'd then have to break into the cinema's office.

He picks up the receiver. He's here. In the office of the cinema behind the pried-open door. Chaplin and Kid, Marilyn Monroe, Marlon Brando and James Dean — they all watch him from their posters. The phone rings.

A long ring . . . where are you, my friend?

You wouldn't believe it! Such a strange thing's happened to me, I want to show myself a movie, come to . . . right now, because I'm depressed, but if you can't, could you please tell me how to work a projector?

Rrinng, Rrrinnng!

Nothing. Just long ringing.

And then the man dials another number, but not at random. And on the other end a somnolent yet surprised voice replies.

"Hi, Dad!

"I'm here.

"In the cinema.

"I'm waiting for you.

"I'm here again."

I, city, can do nothing other than wait.

I sit in the front row. Who comes to the confined man first? His father, or the usherettes who ring with their keys and call the police?

an appearance, intercity

If there is something to envy me, then it's my appearance, intercity, because my appearance, intercity, is a
road. And not just any road, but the road of an iron
horse, who for the needs of civilization converted itself
into a tram that rushes between me and Litvínov,
passing that most strange of human creations — a
chemical plant that, because it was established by
Hitler, for a long time after bore Stalin's name.
Thousands of people head daily from Most to
Litvínov, to harness our incredible inheritance from
Hitler and Stalin; they return home unaware of being
heroes, because this nation never fought against Hitler
nor Stalin, and so only the Poles, Ukrainians and
Southern Slavs who come today know what it means
to harness energy that is an inheritance of war.
But the intercity road isn't only traveled by heroes:
hockey fanatics speed along this road, too; they have
yellow-black scarves and sing victory songs: "If we
aren't relegated from the league, we win the league,"
and their scarves, two meters long, are a premiere's red
carpet for the winners of the hockey league, which
once again this year will be the team sponsored by the
chemical plant: hockey players in the most yellow-
black colors of the world, in colors loved by the

Spaniard Joan Miró, a great painter and the greatest
poet of colors, the most famous fan ever of Team
Chemopetrol. Boys also take this road to Canada. You
don't believe me? Every morning at five, woken from
their children's dreams, they chase their dream.
It's not a paradox. They have skates sharp as knives and
jockstraps fit for grown men. These boys don't have
time for childhood, but they know their slapshooters
from the hat-trickers, and what it means to fly to
fortune in Canada. Let's cross our fingers for them —
maybe Wayne Gretzky will smile at them, and give a
onetime wave from the retirees' bench.
On the intercity road rockers ride, too, to the Quite
Small Theater to listen to the quite big second coming
of Janis Joplinka, who tells them that a Mercedes Benz
is for all the queens of flowers, and that ever since the
beginning of the world Blues Bouillon has been given
out not at the rallies before elections, but at the
reunions, where heroes are heroes, children children,
flowers flowers and blues are always to be found in
blue.
Sky blue.

an appearance, telephonic

I'm a city with a radio. Of which I'm very proud. It's good to be a city and to have a radio.

And it's even better to sound into the ether in the voice of a beautiful girl. A broadcaster working at night.

Then, the whole atmosphere of the sleeping city is charged . . . you know with what.

One day, a voice calls on the appeal of the beautiful broadcaster: "Yes, my friends, how very much would I like to be with you on this June night. What are you doing right now, what are you dreaming of? Do you dream in color?

"Or, you know what? Call me, and tell me what you're doing right now on this balmy night."

And a voice, which will join the voice of the charming broadcaster at 90.6, will state:

"You asked me what I'm doing right now, Ms. Navrátilová? I'm sleeping. With you . . ."

Is it the voice of a pervert? you ask, if you, too, listen to the radio at night. Or maybe a young man in love? But you know what?

I'm not answering any questions.

I'm a city, and I can telephone to the ether whatever I want.

an appearance, sadomasochistic

Spanish flies. The beautiful urge to pleasure.
Hymenoptera. Female hymenopteran. Male
hymenopteran.

They halved them, too. After a divorce everything gets
halved, doesn't it? But they were reasonable. They
didn't need an army of lawyers; they didn't need a
court, or Justice with her scales. Justice with her
scales is blind. They had sight; they knew how to halve
Spanish flies.

They stood before the courthouse. It drizzled a bit
when they hugged for the last time, then they went
their separate ways. They didn't look back once. God
knows how smart they were, they thought. How they
turned out all right in the end. Men and women in
their situation do terrible things in court.

Luckily for them capital punishment had been
abolished here.

O, my dear Marquis de Sade.

Luckily for them the punishment of slavery had been
abolished here, too. But the heroes of my story were
street-smart. World-wise. They were civilized like the
courtesans of Rome.

"It's just a job," said a wench to the Empress
Messalina, "not my joy. Above all I love flowers,

because they are Platonic!"

They were platonic, too. Above all, they were in love with their style.

Flagellating with divorce was as alien to them as flagellating with sex. O, dear Marquis de Sade. They simply split as men and women split before the public toilets.

He would go to the Boys' and she to the Girls'.

Only a deviant would confuse them.

To pay heed to the call of nature, they righteously divided everything they had acquired in the six years of their marriage. How smart they were. And how foolish. Halved Spanish flies will no longer fly to pleasure.

And the shells picked up in that bay in Yugoslavia, they halved them, too. Then they went home and listened. But the halved ocean doesn't murmur.

Could be that war in the bay . . .

an appearance, caffeinated

I love coffee. It's the vice of the cities. They make it
from the night. I make it, too. Sometimes for breakfast
I take it light. I sweeten it at other times, when my
people kiss in their bedrooms at night — because those
nights are sweet. Believe me.

I like all people who drink coffee. Such people I gladly
smell, and listen to their pulse, and I believe them
when they tell the future from the grinds.

One day, I sat down on a bench at the bus station. I
didn't want to go anywhere. A city can't just uproot
itself and take off to Prague whenever it wants to.
What would come of it?

Seventy thousand deserted!

But as I say, I wasn't going anywhere.

I only inhaled the coffee from the plastic cup of a man
who was sad, because he was drinking filtered coffee,
without grinds, and so he didn't know a thing about his
future. He was convinced his future had ended a long
time ago; that he was just the fossilized remains of a
mammoth. On the nearby bench sat a beautiful young
Gypsy woman, but the man would never have had the
courage to ask her about his future.

Even the slyest Gypsy isn't able to prophesize from the
hands of people who have no future.

And so he just sat; he actually wasn't going anywhere, or waiting for anyone, he wasn't studying any schedule in order to find his way through life. He only drank coffee dully. The young Gypsy girl was of an entirely different order than the dark Gadjo. She was wearing an orange sweater and blue jeans. Rings with Czech garnets were like her lips. Lashes like brushes. She would paint her husband's body with them, if she had a husband.

She didn't. He let himself be read of his future, gave her a child and fled. The future had frightened him.

The two people sat, each in their own universe, each on their own bench.

They would never have met, if the stirrer of the story hadn't happened to be hatred.

What an idiotic human quality.

A woman in a duffle coat, holding parcels in paper fastened with thick twine, came to the Gypsy's bench. She laid into the Gypsy in a shrill voice: she's nothing more than filth, defiling the entire country, she ought to go off to India or even further away, she ought to make an appointment with Hitler and the Nuremberg laws . . .

The petite Gypsy woman stood up.

"Please," she asked the man, "could I sit next to you?"

"Yes, of course," the man replied.

"That lady shouted at me as if I were a Gypsy . . ." the

girl explained shyly, "but I actually don't know if I am. My father's name was Fernando Mattinelli."

"Ma–tti–ne–lli?" the man sang.

"But that sounds Spanish or Italian.

"And what if you were! Man, if I were a Gypsy, I wouldn't be sitting here drinking coffee. Ha, to have hot blood. Hell, even my coffee's gone cold!"

"It wouldn't bother you," Miss Mattinelli smiled, "even if I were?"

"As long as it doesn't bother you that I have a hard time getting a tan. I get freckles like someone was shitting on me through a fan."

"And what would you do if you were a Gypsy?" asked Miss Mattinelli.

"Well, first thing I would go to a house in Jiřetín, take a knife and slit the throats of all the rabbits there," said the man.

"For God's sake, why would you do something like that?" She was appalled.

"Anything's better than sitting here . . . anyway . . ." the man waved his hand.

"Those rabbits do you any harm?" Miss Mattinelli asked in a whisper.

"To hell with harm — they only made me happy, nibbling away at their alfalfa, and I fed them dandelion leaves through the grating . . ."

"So then what?"

"Well, they belonged to a friend of mine who asked me to take care of them while he went away, and while I was taking care of them he was off with my wife. Soon enough, my family was reproducing like rabbits." The man gave a sigh.

"You too, mister? You also were trusting? I'm not the only one to have cherished a viper at my breast?" The Gypsy was incensed. "When I'm with a man, I banish all others from my head, and only that one, well — I give him everything; I want him to be in heaven with me; you know what I mean by heaven, don't you? My momma told me it was my own fault that he left me for that fat waitress from the Astoria winebar — that it's my fault I bathed him, I rubbed him with towels, I perfumed him for me and brought him everything he could ever want, right in front of his nose, like no waitress would ever do . . ."

"I have to tell you, Miss Mattinelli, you scare me. I've never been to this heaven you're talking about. I worked like an ox with those rabbits, while another licked cream and another made my children."

"Wow!" Miss Mattinelli burst into laughter, "*another made my children*, that's great."

"Now even you're laughing about it," sighed the man, "and you don't even know my name. You are Mattinelli, your father was Fernando; no one would confuse you with anyone else; but I'm Novák. How many Nováks are there? Even the father of my children is Novák. How easy it was for my wife. She was and stayed Nováková. Terrible, no?"

The man quieted and looked at Miss Mattinelli. But Miss Mattinelli immediately knew what to say to that, and she did: "Your father was Novák and that's why you're Novák. I wanted to be named Markowiczová after my mother, but Momma screamed at me: Your father loved you, so you'll be Mattinelli and that's the end of it. You see my father died the same day I was born. He celebrated my birth with friends, and then they rode drunk in a car. At a crossing, they were hit by a train. My father could have loved me only one day."

"Damn," was all Mr. Novák could say, remembering his own father. He looked at the Gypsy. He noticed that she had a picture in a frame, suspended at her waist on a belt. The picture was turned upside down and Mr. Novák became very curious.

"What do you have there?" he asked Miss Mattinelli. "I'll show it to you," the Gypsy spoke in a whisper, "but only after . . ."

"After what?" Mr. Novák asked with trepidation. "After I read your fate from your hand," answered Miss Mattinelli, "I know how to do that. In that I'm a real Gypsy." And at once she took Mr. Novák's hand, so fast that he couldn't protest. His sleeve slid up and revealed a wrist.

It showed her the seam of a suicide attempt.

Mr. Novák coughed in embarrassment.

"Your lifeline is long," exclaimed the Gypsy, gazing numbly at the scar, "you can expect a long life, and love with a woman who will finally take you to heaven. You'll be the happiest man and you'll have plenty of your own children."

"All right, Miss Mattinelli, now show me the picture," he requested, and she untied the frame from her waist, turned it around and showed him the front, where there was a photograph of a one-year-old girl in a pink dress. "Marcelka. Mine. A hundred-fifty tiny dresses she has in the closet. Everything I buy is only for her. Who else? But when I have a man, oh, he'll be happy — Marcelka doesn't need so many dresses and in the closet there's still so much space."

As Miss Mattinelli said that, she raised her hands and conjured something enormous in the air — perhaps it was a closet, or something else, but as she raised her arms above her head and her bosom pressed up against the orange sweater, Mr. Novák recognized that he had to take a deep drink down to the bottom of the coffee so as not to pass out, because he wanted to enjoy this dream fully conscious.

"And you really don't mind that my blood isn't hot enough to knife rabbits, and instead I mutilate myself?" asked Mr. Novák, and Miss Mattinelli shook her head.

And so they got up, the two of them, and because
Mr. Novák wasn't going anywhere, but Miss Mattinelli
was, he stood on the platform, waved after her and
shouted:

"Goodbye, Miss Mattinelli, I will come to see you and
Marcelka soon. Goodbye!"

But because he hadn't asked Miss Mattinelli's name, he
started running after the bus and screamed:

"Your name, Miss Mattinelli, your name . . ."

And she screamed back to him, her mouth pursed out
the window: "Andrea . . . Andrea Mattinelli! And you,
Mr. Novák?!"

Mr. Novák stopped, giddily panting, and when he
finally got his breath back, he roared his name after
the disappearing bus throughout the entire bus station:
"Josef . . . Josef Novák!"

And the old lady, dozing with her parcels on the occupied bench, woke up: "What's going on? Why are you
screaming?"

"I have to scream, Ma'am. Today I was reborn. You are
entirely repulsive, but I'll kiss you all the same. Today,
you saved me from misery!"

And he kissed the old hag and for the whole night he
stayed awake, drinking with me, city, the sweet coffee
of night.

an appearance, military

You ask how the Warsaw Pact could dissolve from one
day to the next? Without the firing of a single shot and
without the shedding of a single drop of blood?
I'll try to explain it to you.
There is a house for dancing, whose floor plan forms
the letter T. "T" like the trot the house was once built
for. Trees grow in front of the house, poplars toward
the heights, rowans toward the blood. A beautiful
house on Podžatecká Street.
It used to be the Railwaymen's Dancing Club in 1987,
the year the military overlords inducted the recruitment classes born in 1967 and 1968.
And because the dancing didn't make full use of the
house throughout the day — during the day only the
Krishnas, the Dervishes and the great ballet-master
Vlastimil Harapes danced there — rolling army induc-
tions for the Warsaw Pact took place here from an
early hour.
The class of 1967. The class of 1968. Boys from the
Gymnasium, technical college, vocational schools,
crowded into the lavatory stalls with their sample cups
and stood over the porcelain bowls. Unfortunates.
They've stood for an hour already, fifty conscripts
above the urinals. And nothing. And more and more of

them coming. A hundred boys. A hundred-fifty. And nothing, still. They stand in confused silence above their empty cups.

They might have stood there until Judgment Day, trying to drink the water from the tap, thinking hard about their early childhoods and their potty-training, and trying somehow to coax their bladders into compliance, if He hadn't come. Dezider Balogh.

A mining apprentice. A middle heavyweight boxer from Baník Most. Such a stud that he'd easily jump rope for an hour, box with his shadow for another hour and dance around the punching bag for yet another hour and a half, all without breaking a sweat. Not until he went to the sauna for two hours could he be seen with a wet forehead.

Such was Dezider Balogh, a middle heavyweight boxer, who in greeting offered his left, not that he was left-handed, but with his right he would crush your hand and cause incredible problems in the network of all those small bones, which enable you to play the piano, construct model airplanes or snap your fingers at a waitress. I tell you, I am a city of reinforced concrete, but I wouldn't step into the ring with Dezider Balogh and his right.

And because Dezider was not scared of any competitor, he approached the bowl with the cup and filled both containers to the brim. One-hundred-eighty conscripts were astounded. Suddenly one of them, bold Mikoláš Smetana, had the idea to hand his container to Dezider.

And Dezider, who feared no rival, filled up the second cup, too. And that day he filled exactly one-hundred-eighty-three of them.

No one else in the world could manage that.

He simply stood, taking the cups from the inductees and passed urine to them. Bravo, Dezider! I applaud, full of admiration even today, after so many years. The hundred-eighty-three young men remember him with gratitude, too.

That's the whole story. I have nothing more to say. Dezider Balogh had bilirubin in his urine. They didn't draft him.

Such a sly pisser!

an appearance, empty

The house is empty — will we make love or cry?
Where did I hear such a question?
Was it in the villa in the Zahražany district, or in that
Márquez book, *One Hundred Years of Solitude*?
And yet it was heard from the villa in Zahražany.
Germans had lived there earlier. Roland from a
photograph in a Wehrmacht uniform — a Christmas
postcard home, he smiles in the photograph, ah yes,
he's still smiling; he doesn't know he's been dead such
a long time.
Auntie Rachel knits mittens for the Eastern Front; she
keeps records of packages sent to Russia, *Winterhilfe*
. . . "today, I sent fifty pairs of gloves to . . ." the
writing is still legible for those who know German,
but no one reads it anymore. On the lone table in the
middle of the otherwise empty room stands a framed
portrait of a great man.
An old man with a white beard. He smiles. And yet
he too is dead. His granddaughter gazes at the photograph and cries. If grandfather had lived, today he
would have been one-hundred years old.
The granddaughter is a bit over twenty and she has
brought her boyfriend to this forsaken house to make
love. Now she cries.

"The beds were here, and there a chest of drawers, the commode . . . and pictures, dishes, cutlery . . . and my grandmother's clock, who could have done that, who would have dared!" With tears in her eyes the girl looks around the plundered villa of her grandfather, the man from the portrait, who came after the war to revive the house.

"Gypsies!" the girl's boyfriend announced.

He didn't want to tell her that in the garden he'd found the hideous carcass of a dog the thieves had eaten. Flies sat on the dog's skin. To banish those awful images, he looked again at the photograph of the old man. No, he couldn't make love with the grand-daughter of such a great man, not here. After all, he thinks, I don't even reach up to his ankles.

"This is a real man! I felt like running away from this weird sickening world as soon as I saw those flies, but he'd survived the Gestapo and the end of the war and a life nearly a hundred years long! And these hoodlums, they didn't even have the respect to leave him in peace."

It doesn't scare him as much that they stole things — pictures, jewelry, dressers — but that in doing so they stole the souls of strangers. They'd violated what was most private, what had remained of that white-haired old man, of Roland and Rachel.

They had brutally raped the house in Zahražany.

When will that question be heard again?
"Will we make love or cry?"
When will my night visitors, the young man and the
young woman, lose their inhibitions and fear?
When will they become naked and merge in embrace,
to fill the empty house in Zahražany with spirit?
I don't know.
I don't believe anything.

an appearance, walking

If I haven't told you about Till yet, about my son from Mozartova Street, then I have to set it right immediately. Because there was always something with this Till.
He was going on twenty-three and had yet to serve in the army. He downright avoided his service.
Fact is he liked to take leave every day. Whenever he wanted.
He just walked the city without a care in the world, looking at whatever he wanted to and either whistled or not.
And once, at Rozkvět, at the shop where Mr. Pivo always has his street show and juggles bottles for a beer — and don't think Mr. Pivo's a small beer, they know him even in Prague, where he used to guest on Národní třída, opposite the Máj department store — Till met a man who walked in a way that seemed as if he almost wasn't able to walk at all: the man leaned against the glass of a shop window and seemed he wouldn't get to wherever it was he was headed.
Till took charge and offered him his arm.
He learned a few facts about the walker that amazed him. The man himself began to mention them:
"You know, young man, I'm going to the tram. I live in

Litvínov, but I was here to go to the cinema. They were showing a film about the Vietnam War. Are you interested in the Vietnam War?" the man asked.

"Hm," Till replied, "Hair, hippies, Jane Fonda, *Coming Home*, Coppola *Apocalypse Now*, Jim Morrison . . . you know, I have to say that I am."

"They got it all wrong, they did, otherwise they couldn't have lost, could they?!" the man reasoned.

"You know, I'm very interested in war. I reported for the first one, in 1914, but they didn't take me."

"What?" Till was shocked. "Mister, would you tell me how old you are?"

"Ninety-nine," the man remarked, "I was nineteen then. I had weak lungs."

"In the Second World War, I was again just a spectator of the newsreels," the combative man complained.

"Well, maybe they'll give you another chance come the Fourth World War," Till thought, "when after the Third they'll have to replenish their manpower."

"But they went about it all wrong," the man continued, "those Americans in the movie, they did . . ."

He could barely crawl, he was ninety-nine years old, but he still wanted to go to war.

Till was enraptured by him.

An immortal man, who would like nothing better than to fall.

an appearance, dancing

Would you like to hear a story about dancing lessons
and first love? C'mon! I know you've heard plenty of
them! But I'll tell you something quite different,
original, not so banal . . . though, when I think about
it, it's unavoidable — the heart of this story is really
first love.

We begin with a joke, as the dancing-master Roubíček
begins the evening lessons for the youth.

"Do you know the one about the lords?" Master
Roubíček screams at the sweating young men in suits,
who look like guests at a Sicilian wedding, their
expressions as if a vendetta as they step the basics of
the jive, polka, and waltz.

"I'll kill him, guys," the young Werther says.

"It's sorry, having to stomp cabbage while listening to
his wisecracks."

But Master Roubíček, as if he hasn't heard him, knows
that his jokes are meant for the young ladies. He perks
up and says: one–two–three and two–two–three, he
claps, showing the slow, unsure and hunched boys
what a true gentleman looks like: always with the most
beautiful debutante, an excellent tie, a perfect body
and, because every evening before going to sleep he
doesn't pick at his pimples as do the participants in

his course, he has the time to invite such beautiful debutantes home.

There is one sorrow more to be experienced by our young Werther.

He dances with the master's assistant, Bešta. Werther is, so to speak, unpaired, surplus.

Roubíček demonstrates dances with Werther's female partner.

Petr Bešta is God's elect. Only two years older than Werther, but already graduated from the beginners' lessons, he has joined the advanced ballroom dancing group. And today? Today he dances body-to-body with the most beautiful girls left to him by Roubíček. Because he's eighteen, he's growing into a master himself. His suit fits like a glove, the fuzz below his nose embarrassing no one, his posture perfect.

He lives in the same building as the young Werther, at the same entrance, and because in the evening after dancing lessons he goes home with his younger friend, on the way he tries to teach him moves of the subtlest finesse.

"Look man, you can't turn with me on one spot all the time; dance is a sophisticated motion Jirka," Petr Bešta explains to his partner.

"You have to sweep the corners with me!"

And so Jirka Werther sweeps corners with him, but so wildly that the next lesson the desperate Bešta screams:

"Slow down, you're throwing me around like Švanda the bagpiper, and I'm just a frail girl . . ." But young Werther sets his teeth, because he can't imagine Bešta being a beautiful girl, and while dancing he whispers infuriated into his partner's ear: "I'll always be sadistic when dancing with you until you and Roubíček give me a girl!"

And Roubíček with his absolute musical pitch hears his name and immediately starts up: "Two English lords are in the restroom, silently urinating next to one another, and when they're about to leave one says to the other: 'Sir, they taught us at Oxford to wash our hands after using the *pissoir*!' And the other replies: 'At Cambridge, they taught us not to piss them . . .' "

"I'll kill him, I'll kill that guy," young Werther hisses over Bešta's shoulder in a caracole, and observes how Roubíček laughs at his own joke and coos with a beautiful debutante. "This is what they call dancing lessons' first love? I swear by all that is sacred that no one will see me here ever again, dancing with a man like some prospector out in the Klondike!"

Once again, young Werther and Bešta Petr go home together in the evening. They stop in front of the house by the garbage cans.

"Man, Bešta, I have problems with the waltz — whenever I begin one I end up in a polka . . ."

"I know," Bešta smiles and goes and stands with his

chest thrust forth like a pigeon, then executes the
Metamorphosis of Bešta into a female partner. And so
the two dancers hold each other at the garbage cans
and dance *On the Beautiful Blue Danube* all the way
inside and up the stairs.

And one–two–three, two–two–three . . .

"Bešta, we look like idiots, don't we?"

"Don't worry, no one's looking."

But it's not true. I, city, am watching.

Laughing, the whole city looks on.

an appearance, fast

Hours and hours I'm able to observe the children's games and to admire how children manage, totally without ostentation, with only a wing-beat of imagination, to change the world.

Take for instance a sandpit.

An ordinary sandpit. And all of a sudden, I see an automobile racetrack: Monza with its chicanes, Nürburgring with its deadly curve, Hungaroring with the long home-stretch. And at the starting-post, in the first row, Gilles Villeneuve, the incomparable, the fastest, the Flying Canadian, as the sportswriters have nicknamed him.

Death or victory, such speed is borne by his plate.

Boys from the house have marbles: red — Ferrari, blue — Ligier, yellow — canary Fittipaldi, black — Lotus, white — Williams, every marble a hero of their childhood. But Toník has the greatest red hero; he has the Flying Canadian, Gilles Villeneuve, and so it's no wonder that Toník plays so perfectly, that he's already won nine Grands Prix, that the whole sandpit lies at his feet. He turns past even the most difficult chicane without collision, even in the most fierce encounter with his competitors he keeps a cool head. He, Toník, death or victory.

"That'd be something if Villeneuve came to the track at Most, wouldn't it?" says Zdeněk, Niki Lauda to his friends.

"No way, dude . . ." gasps Toník, aka Gilles Villeneuve.

"The guy doesn't even know the Most track exists!" says Roman, Nelson Piquet.

"What about writing to him?" suggests Libor, Clay Regazzoni.

"And how, idiot, in Czech?" laughs Víťa, James Hunt.

"Bullshit — in Canada they speak French, English or Indian," reasons Ríša, Alain Prost.

"And you know any of those?" asks Niki Lauda.

"Well, Indian, a couple of words. Methane-aqua, for instance," boasts Alain Prost.

"What the hell does that mean?" asks Gilles Villeneuve.

James Hunt erupts in maniacal laughter.

"Well . . . a lightning-fast knife," replies a perplexed Alain Prost.

"Dumbass!" Niki Lauda adds.

"Hey, don't call him names, what do you know? Since when you are so smart?" Alain Prost protests.

"Me? Definitely not Indian, retard!"

"Who you calling retard, you son of a bitch!"

"Craphead!"

"Assface!"

"Toothless cunt!"

"Scumbag!"

"All of you shut up," Gilles Villeneuve jumps in between the friends, already beginning to fight. "We can write the letter in Czech and give it to our teacher Mrs. Jonášová to translate!"

"Well, yeah, that'd do," admits Niki Lauda.

"Ok. Ok. Ok." The boys all agree.

In a few weeks, all the boys are waiting tensely for an answer. The teacher was a bit surprised, though, but when they introduced themselves and told her who Villeneuve and Niki Lauda were, and so on, she gladly translated the letter. She even found the address of the Grand Prix Drivers Association, chaired by Mr. Bernie Ecclestone.

In short, she was a fine woman.

All agreed that when Villeneuve comes to the Most track, they damn well better invite Teach.

"Jesus, Villeneuve . . ." screams Víťa.

"Goddamn right, vroooom . . ." exults Libor.

"Gentlemen, in Most . . ." Zdeněk cries.

Toník silently daydreams about the Flying Canadian at the track in Most.

About going to see him in the depot, bringing him to sign all the cuttings from the car magazines that he's glued with care into his big notebook with the F-1s. And then Gilles Villeneuve would take off, and again he'd be the fastest, because that's the way it is. Simple as that. He's the greatest hotshot. Everyone else can eat his dust.

Toník's dreamy fever rises each day. Motorcycle, off-road vehicle, and truck races are held on the track in Most, and he goes to see them all only because he waits for Villeneuve, for the only true champion.

Until one day. In the first poll position is Gilles Villeneuve, next to him Niki Lauda, followed by Clay Regazzoni and James Hunt. Their engines are warming up, the green light of the starting semaphore will light up at any moment, the tension rises . . . and, in that moment, Alain Prost runs to the sandpit behind the house, out of breath and screaming:

"Guys, Villeneuve got killed, Villeneuve got killed, yesterday, Mother saw it all on TV!"

And silence. All of a sudden — a silence I haven't heard the likes of in years. All are looking at Toník, the best marbles player of the Most Grand Prix, the greatest racer of the children's sandpit.

Toník bends down for the red clay marble and throws it out of the pit. It falls in the grass, but they all see where. Only no one dares pick it up.

For a while, Toník sits with his head on his knees. No one says anything. I don't make a sound.

Such silence that one can hear the grass grow around the thrown marble.

And then Toník gets up.

He runs to the marble quickly. He picks it up and returns it to the racetrack.

"Who are you?" asks Zdeněk, Niki Lauda.

"Gilles Villeneuve," Toník replies.

I told this story to Jacques Villeneuve, Formula 1 driver, and he said to me: "Yes, in my previous life I was a father, and now I'm a son."

And then both of us admired the imagination of children — able to come up with games that are immortal.

an appearance, theological

When next you go to the museum, try to ask the collections' curator to see a letter that the pope, John Paul II, addressed to me, the city of Most.

The pope's letters are traditionally called encyclicals and the head of the Church references them only to matters of global importance. In his letters you won't find glosses such as "Agnieszka, I love you," and if you do, then be sure that they're intended only and solely to Agnes Přemyslid in the year of her canonization. And so I am proud to own such a letter, which refers to me personally and with its impassionate Catholic conveyance uplifts me unto the heavens. How did it come that John Paul II sat down and wrote an encyclical to me in particular? Let yourselves be told!

It was the day before Christmas Eve, Year of Our Lord one thousand nine hundred and ninety six, when the pastor of the Deacon's Church of the Annunciation of the Virgin Mary, Doctor of Theology Koukl, had to visit Doctor Říčan, the chief physician of orthopedics at the hospital of Most.

It all happened this way: the doctor of theology had gazed at the starry sky above him so unfortunately that he slipped on the icy ground and broke his leg. Of course, Dr. Říčan fixed his leg, but it took a couple of operations and a long period of recovery, and so it was unthinkable that the pastor would be able to officiate for his parishioners at Midnight Mass on Christmas Eve.

Where was a substitute to be found so quickly? Priests, there are precious few of them, and all already had arranged their stints for the season, and so Th.D. Koukl called his sacristan from the hospital: "Cancel the midnight. Due to contemplation, stargazing, slipping, icy ground and leg, I won't be able to make it. Do you understand? Repeat it, Sacristan."

"Cancel the midnight. Due to contemplation, stargazing, icy ground and leg you can't make it. I understand," repeated Charouz the sacristan.

And because right at that time Sacristan Charouz was being visited by Mr. Kolyně and Mr. Látal, the latter repeated after the sacristan:

"What's that, Mr. Charouz? Due to contemplation, stargazing, slipping, icy ground and leg the midnight is canceled? Incredible!"

"What's that, through leg, stars, icy ground and contemplation the Christians will be short a feast of God? That's terrible!" Mr. Kolyně lamented.

Both men were very pious and every Sunday and Friday they assembled for mass at the House of the City of Cherson. They also frequently visited Sacristan Charouz and with him they would dispute which was better, the Catholic or Evangelical faith.

From this, it should be evident that they were both faithful Evangelicals.

"Well, I'll call off the altar boys and the choir," said the sacristan and reached for the telephone again.

And suddenly Mr. Kolyně had an idea: "Don't call off anyone, Sacristan — we'll celebrate the mass!"

The sacristan was stupefied. "Who we?" he asked.

"Well, the two of us," Mr. Kolyně declared and pointed a finger at himself and Mr. Látal.

"Sure," agreed Mr. Látal, "no problem at all."

"You know how to do it?" The sacristan shook his head in disbelief.

"You see . . . if you'd listened to our explanations about the Evangelical faith, you'd have long known that every Evangelical is himself a bit of a theologian and priest, since everyone in our Church can lead a mass and interpret the Gospel. Our Church is democratic, for Luther said: 'Don't create a nobility to approach God. You must all take responsibility for the interpretation of the Word. You must all take up weapons in the fight against the power of Satan!'" Mr. Látal admonished the sacristan.

"Do you understand?"

"No, gentlemen," the sacristan shook his head.

"Never mind. What's important now is to show us where the venerable pastor keeps the vestments, the sacramental wine, the monstrance and the chalice."

"And you would really celebrate it, boys?" The sacristan was delighted.

"Without a doubt."

"Don't even ask!"

They kept their word.

People, I am only an ordinary city. I'm neither the Vatican nor Rome. Nothing seemed strange to me at Midnight Mass.

Nothing unusual. That the congregation in addition to the Host got a little nip of wine? Let them have a good time. Isn't it Christmas?

But the singing from the choir, the scent of the incense, the vestments and the reading from the Holy Bible — all that was as usual. Having mass celebrated by two pastors was perhaps a bit out of the ordinary, but since when have the two of them been so polite?! Like true gentlemen, each gave way to the other:

"Nay, Sir Pastor, you read now, oh no, Sir Pastor, your sermon has priority, after you doctor, no, after you . . ."

And the people who attended this Midnight Mass in the Deacon's Church of the Annunciation of the Virgin Mary left inspired by the Holy Ghost and by a grand sense of community:

"After you, madam, after you, sir," they were saying on their way out the gates of the church, rather than pushing as usual.

And because Mr. Kolyně and Mr. Látal then boasted so much of their achievement in competent Catholic circles, the Holy Father in the Vatican sat himself down upon a Renaissance tabouret and wrote an encyclical of this wording, mangling his native Polish in an attempt at communicating in Czech:

Czech people, please to lose your Hussite tendencies, John Paul II, to Most, City in Bohemia, A.D. 1997.

And because the pope's encyclical came into the hands of the mayor of Most, who had originally been a historian, he responded to John Paul in return: "Dear Sir, to Your official breve from the twelfth of this month I — with the power of my position, and also of my profession — am authorized to state that the city of Most has never been Hussite, for our population in those days was one-hundred percent German."
And John Paul responded with these words:

Then, sir, please to lose your Lutheranism too!

an appearance, grave

Some appearances people would gladly forbear. I
understand. No one wants to be buried alive. Luckily,
the dead don't seem to care. Or do they? Do they
come back, dead among the living, perhaps even in an
altered appearance, to carry out their cruel jokes? Do
they return?

Yes, they do. I, city, saw a dead man, who came back
twice, and in altered appearance, to interfere in the
fate of his son.

His son, I should point out, was alive.

Listen . . .

It was raining. A downpour so bad that one wouldn't
let out the dog.

A gray curtain was lowered over the cemetery.

The planet rotated in a slow pilgrimage through the
universe like an old locomotive short of wind.

Somebody stoked the boiler; the chimney of the
crematorium puffed away, its smoking hanging low
to the ground, below the gray clouds.

How was Tony feeling, listening to the eulogy for his
father in the funeral hall?

What was going on inside him as a raindrop on the
steamed-up glass slowly rode down and a second,

faster drop took to pursue it, catching up with it to create a small private sea?

"This man always took excellent care of his family. So often did he sacrifice his time for the happiness and safety of his fellow man! Many times was he to deny himself the benefits of his career to create instead a private paradise for the sake of his children . . ."

When a tear pursues another tear and overtakes it, they create a small private sea. Because tears are salty, thought Tony.

Eva, Tony's girlfriend, clutched her boyfriend's hand. What is he thinking about, she thought.

"A man who was without exception honest, open, friendly and tolerant. To his wife, he was not just a husband, but also a friend, an advisor, a father, a brother . . ." the orator spoke.

Incest, thought Tony.

Eva, Tony's girlfriend, caressed her boyfriend's palm. She traced his lifeline; such a long, long way, she mused, from the embryo to the grave.

"He never drank, he ate in moderation, he kept himself in shape. He also encouraged his son to take up sports, and fully experienced all his athletic successes and failures. He knew how to face failure like a man. For example, when he came in last in the Jizerská 50, he was able to shake hands sportingly with all his forty-nine betters . . ."

What's he babbling about? Tony thought. Since when was the Jizerská 50 named for having fifty participants? Is he desperate? Eva scrutinized her boyfriend. Does he resemble his father? What do I like most about him? Maybe the fact that I don't really know him? That I never really know what he thinks?

"Farewell, husband, father and brother!" the funeral director finished his speech and sent the coffin down the elevator and into the flames.

"God," Tony let slip.

Eva released Tony's hand, so he could accept the condolences.

"Accept my sympathy, accept my sympathy . . ." the people who had known his father were saying. He didn't know any of them. He actually didn't know his father either. He didn't know he had raced in the Jizerská 50, or that he'd loved his family.

"My father was the biggest son of a bitch I ever knew," he whispered to Eva, "he boozed, he beat my mother and me . . ."

"Ah," Eva breathed.

"I feel terrible . . . Accept my sympathy," she said and pressed Tony's lifeline.

Tony was glad she was pressing. He decided to tell her he loved her, that he had been afraid to marry her and have a child with her, but that now he wasn't afraid anymore, that he wanted it, that here and now he wants it, and, if she agrees, he would go with her to her parents and ask them for her hand and that then they would go to city hall, to the church and to bed; they would go there, straight from this sad place, and they would say yes twice and throw caution to the wind and . . .

What next, he didn't know. The funeral director was pulling his sleeve, tugging at the thread of his dream. "Mister, mister," the frightened director shouted, "a terrible thing's happened, I have to tell you!"

"Yes, I know," said Tony, "you've just laid my father to rest."

"Actually no, mister. Pardon me. It was all a mistake! "A huge mistake. It wasn't your father who was just laid to rest!"

"What?" Tony was frightened. "Who was it then?"

"It was Mr. Majer, Mr. Oleksevič. Your father's turn's now," the director confessed, tail between his legs.

"Hahahaha," Tony began laughing, "ha ha . . . so then the one you eulogized was really the philanthropist, the teetotaler, the sportsman and the loving father. Well, the whole thing did seem strange to me," Tony said with tears streaming from his eyes. One after another. Salty. A small private sea.

"I'm sorry," the director shrugged his shoulders.

"You know what?" Tony asked the man.

"Forget it. My father's relatives and acquaintances

have already left. Let it lie. When you're going to bury my real father, feel free to repeat what you just said to Mr. Majer's relatives. It's done. I won't trouble you about it anymore."

The director relaxed, and smiled with humility.

"You are understanding, Mr. Oleksevič. Truly understanding."

As Tony and his girlfriend turned to leave he made a mean grimace at their backs, and smacked his forehead:

"You think I'd talk differently about your real pop? It's scripted the same way for everyone. Only the names change. You worm!

"You don't know that one only speaks well of the dead?"

He rushed off for the soul of Mr. Majer, dragging his hoof behind him.

"Hahahaha," he laughed darkly.

Yet Tony was not able to leave. He stood in the rain behind the glass like one of those drops chasing another and watched his real father now. His way into the flames. He heard from behind the glass neither music nor sounds, it was a silent movie. With Buster Keaton. What's he have on his mind now? Eva asked herself. Her skin was soaked. The rain denuded her, not the tears. Tears denude more. But she still had her body. She knew this body was beautiful. She was sure of it. Tony had told her that a thousand times. And if not Tony, then others would always assure her. But she wanted him — for him she would bare herself more than the rain ever could. She loved him. Though she didn't know why him in particular. Maybe because his lifeline was so long! So terribly long, that she herself secretly called it IMMORTALITY.

"Come on," Tony said. The fish-tank ceremony had ended. The smoke from the chimney made the planet with its gray and heavy clouds run from the west to the east.

"Yes, dear," she agreed. She saw that he wanted to tell her something. Now, she said to herself, wet to the bone and happy, now, and lifted her face to him so that he could see she was waiting, that she could, and only for him, finally say it.

Tony drew a breath and everything he had committed himself to could have been said in that moment. If for a second time his father hadn't weighed in. Now no longer as Majer, but as another substance.

Soot fell from the chimney of the crematorium onto the girl's face. As if a Madame De Pompadour's beauty spot, the soot became enthroned on her cheek.

All of a sudden, Tony couldn't take his eyes off it. He took such a long look he forgot how to talk.

He forgot to say he loved her, that he had been afraid to marry her and to have a child with her, but that now he wasn't afraid anymore, that he wanted it, that here and now he wants it, and that if she agrees, he would go with her to her parents and ask them for her hand and then they would go to city hall, and to the church; they would go there, straight from this sad place, and they would say yes twice.

He didn't say that. He only bowed to Eva's cheek and blew away the soot.

They have never spoken of it since.

This is the way a cemetery sometimes buries love.

And not only the love of the dead, but also that of the living.

an appearance, tame

Every time the Berolina Circus came to visit me and
pitched its brightly colored tent full of tiny light bulbs
perching along its ridges like swallows on a wire, the
Stankov family found themselves in an argument. The
argument was always about who would go to the
evening show with the children, Robert, Kryštof, and
Daniel from around the block. Who would take these
three rascals ages six, seven and nine, to the Park at
the End of the Line, to the rounded ground under the
big-top.
Who would buy them cotton candy, pistachio ice
cream, taffy and those fake noses on elastic strings.
Who would slap them when they spat at the tigers.
(*Actually, the adults don't know this, but the children
always spit at the tamer, cowardly hiding behind his tigers!*)
Who would explain to them there's no need to be
scared and cry when the clowns kick themselves in the
butt, that it's all actually one big joke. And then when
they'd break up in laughter, who could bear it? Well,
tell me, who?
Mrs. Stankovová resolutely declares:
"Father."
So Mr. Stankov knows that today it's his turn to go.
No arguments apply when it comes to the circus. A

circus isn't a social function, where a woman could put on a chic dress and show herself in a loggia box. The circus is an obnoxious tumult shot through with coarse humor: clowns spit at faces, the magicians from the sideshow force you to participate, though you don't want to, the horses swirl dust, you feel sorry for the poodles, the spangles somehow aren't glamorous enough for the eyes of a lady. And yet Mrs. Stankovová might take her sons to see figure skating, where the sequins don't bother her. It's actually a beautiful dance on ice. But are her boys and Daniel, an orphan from the neighborhood who lives with his grandmother, interested in such dances? They're still too young to appreciate the grace of the girls, and if they see men dancing on ice, they don't mince their words.

They say: "A man should play hockey! These guys are queers!" "Oh, well," sighs Mr. Stankov, who puts on his sports jacket and whistles for the boys.

They go to the circus.

At the circus, the boys behave as they should: they laugh their heads off, they spit at the tigers (*shh, as we know now, at the tamer*), they put away six sticks of cotton candy, six cones of ice cream and six pieces of chewing gum, swallowed.

The Berolina bandmaster gives an Eb. After the tigers comes something unique. The ringmaster himself introduces the new act:

"And now, ladies and gentlemen, a world-famous artist from Bulgaria! Nina Dimitrova and her polar bears.
"A polar bear is an animal that is impossible to tame. As of this moment her wards are still feral, as they were in the Arctic wilderness. These bears have already killed three tamers. But when she enters their cage, they'll do what she wills.
"How will she manage that, you ask? I don't know. It's her secret. It's her. Nina Dimitrova!"
And in come five white polar bears with the fiery Nina Dimitrova: her mighty breasts are laced up in an elaborate corset, her leather pants are tight-fitting, in her hand she holds a whip and above her forehead with its flashing tiara waves thick black hair that reaches down to the middle of her back.
"Dad, Dad, look," Robert and Kryštof scream.
"Mr. Stankov," gasps Daniel.
And the boys and the man then observe how the white beasts grow tender and scurry around Nina Dimitrova, letting themselves be spun around cumbersomely in some kind of high-stepping folk dance, then become a horse for her, next a sofa and a hairdresser's dryer for her hair. For that, Nina Dimitrova combs her hair up into a bun and shoves it all into the maw of a bear breathing hot. And then she pulls her hair out and the bear seems afraid even to dribble. Her hairdo has not been devalued in the least; it's still the snazziest to be

found on our planet. Nina Dimitrova, the most beautiful woman in the world.

Applause. Bravo! Bravo, Nina Dimitrova!

As Nina Dimitrova disappears after her bears, the boys get an idea.

"Dad," Robert asks, "what about us going to ask her how she gets all those untamed bears to obey her?"

"What? Well, okay. Go." Their father approves a bit absent-mindedly. Robert, Kryštof and Daniel sneak behind the scenes, and Kryštof meditates:

"I think Dad's interested too. Imagine if we knew what this woman knows. Then everyone would obey us."

And like the three Magi who, caps in hand, go caroling, Robert, Kryštof, and Daniel approach Nina Dimitrova and chirp: "Madam, please, we . . ."

"O God!" screams the world-famous artist from Bulgaria, threatening them with her polar-bear whip. "Get those damned brats out of here!"

"Surely it was a mistake," Mr. Stankov comforts his sons and Daniel from the neighborhood. They sit in the arena like whipped curs. "You must've gotten confused," he says, "she spoke Bulgarian and you misunderstood. Wait, I'll go see her myself."

"Dad, you know Bulgarian?" asks Robert.

"Sure," he answers.

"Your dad's great," thinks Daniel, "he knows everything in the world."

After an hour of waiting, Robert, Kryštof, and Daniel went to find him. The show had ended a long time ago and they wanted to go home.
"Go on, boys," their father called out at them. He was engaged in convivial talk with Nina Dimitrova, "tell Mom, that . . . that . . . that I'll come right away."
"Your dad knows Bulgarian very well," observed Daniel, when he was parting from both junior Stankovs.
"Well, of course he does," Kryštof agreed. "I only hope that he'll get out of that woman the secret of how she does all that stuff with the bears."
The boys argued for a long time before falling asleep over what kind of a trick it could be, but because they didn't come up with anything, they fell asleep and had dreams in which it all came to them easily.
They hadn't a clue as to when their father returned home from the circus.

"She didn't give it away," Father whispered to the boys in the morning.
"That sucks," the boys thought.
And neither did they notice that for the next two weeks their father was washing the dishes, dusting the whole

house, shining the silver and taking out the trash.
He was doing chores he hated from the depths of his
soul and that he, even in a modern marriage, couldn't
ever find justification for. What had happened? The
boys of course wouldn't know, but Mrs. Stankovová
herself went to Nina Dimitrova for an answer.
And to her, she apparently revealed her secret.
From that moment on, her husband obeys no longer
like a clock, but like a polar bear.
And he has been strictly forbidden from attending the
circus for the next fifty years.

an appearance, silent

Look, up there, as far up as the penultimate floor —
the window. They lived together there. Dreamt. You
see the window-box — there they nurtured it. You
think they had a good crop? Here, amid the apartment
blocks?

Don't be crazy. Even their dreams wilted.

Toward the end they didn't even sing, he sold the
guitar and just lay below the poster of John Lennon,
looking at her pacing the room, looking how she didn't
love him anymore, looking how she seemed to want to
fly away, how she was suffocated. He looked, and
examined the feeling. It was something in A minor
that sounded in his soul, but who would've taken an
interest in it.

Without dreams and without a guitar.

Then she left. She sent a postcard from London.

She took a trip. The second postcard came from
Liverpool. John Lennon.

The young man was still picking up his mail then. Not
anymore. Look, the mailbox is full.

Paul McCartney, Ringo Starr, George Harrison.

But there was no power able to raise him from his bed.
He lay whole days long, she left him a stereo system
and he programmed only one song.

It played through his days and nights, over and over.
It was "Breathing" by Kate Bush. He liked the song
very much. Yes, his girlfriend actually looked a lot like
Kate Bush.
One day, though, the young man had to get up.
The electrician rang, coming to cut off the electricity.
Then the song didn't sound. The neighbors breathed a
sigh of relief. But not for long. One day, the song was
heard again from his studio apartment. The young
man sang it. It sounded like a mantra:
"Breathing . . .
breathing . . . breathing . . .
breathing . . . breathing . . . breathing . . .
breathing . . . breathing."
Understand?
Breathing . . . breathing . . . breathing . . . breathing
. . . over and over again!

an appearance, authentic

It was in my new chapel, there at the old vocational school, now the city museum, where I first saw him. He was immersed in prayer, the material world ceased to exist for him, and I, city, asked myself, what makes him seem so peculiar to me? Yes, immediately afterward I understood. While the believers were shaking hands at the end of the mass, I realized that he was the only young man there.

All the others in God's tabernacle were already old relics, on whose yellow, shriveled and tired faces life had inscribed a goodly number of wrinkles. When they kneeled on the hassock and wrung their hands over their prayers, their knees cracked like wood drying for a Stradivarius violin.

The Lord's Prayer then streamed from their lips like dry leaves drifted away by the wind. They had one leg in the grave and another still at the altar, at least I imagined it that way, and it was a strangely horrific picture for me, like those of Hieronymus Bosch.

The gout, the disease of old legs, washed up on them from the inside, swishing whenever the worms bit into one leg, the other leg held firmly by angels at the altar. But he was young. He stood with both of his feet on firm ground, or with his knees on the hassock, his face turned to the Lord. His prayers weren't dead leaves; his prayers were will. Perhaps that's why God always granted him whatever he asked.

His requests were not small. He wanted to become the richest man in the city. He slept five hours a day and the rest of the time he worked toward fulfilling his dream.

He had his start with the sale of antiques to rich collectors from Germany. Then he discovered that these connoisseurs hungered for old weapons inlaid with gold and silver, the muzzle-loading and breech-loading models from the 18th century, with gun-lock mechanisms, as if they were Prague's astronomical clocks; so he started to produce them — exact replicas, impossible to differentiate from their older brethren. They knew how to kill, but they were beautiful.

So it is with women: they can kill, but they are beautiful, our young man thought. With the capital from the old icons and rifles, he opened a red-light house with young women. He chose the ladies himself. They can kill, but they're beautiful.

At that time, the young man had employees. He signed over the salon to one of them and took all the profits for himself. He accepted art- and conservation-school graduates for his historical-weapons workshop, where they refined his wares according to period engravings and illustrations. He moved the antique shop to

Prague, where he found a much greater market.

Still, every Sunday he came to my chapel, immersing himself in a world free of money and business, continuing to believe in his God. Whenever someone from the local congregation came to him and asked him for money, providing good reason, he gave it. He was no usurer and was not stingy. God, after all, doesn't charge interest.

Don't you believe?

Every Saturday morning you can see him in front of his house washing his Sierra with affectionate care. Stroking it and whispering to it like a lover. How beautiful these cars are. Beautiful, though they can kill. But he was always protected by God. He was protected from the insidiousness of money, too. Millions in the bank never harmed him.

They haven't even changed him. He still wears his worn jeans and there's not a ring on any of his fingers. He despises the boredom of the balls, parties, and happenings; and fortunately the comely debutantes, VIPs, and the intrusive paparazzi of the tabloids don't go to church.

The only ones there are the tired old people, who protect him from pride, and God, his silent and only companion, who doesn't disclose anything of the man's audacious plans to the competition, even though He could, for He knows everything.

an appearance, windy

I've already told you about Till and his walks. Didn't I?
So listen to what happened when Till was nine and
met Gustáv Husák, the president of Czechoslovakia.
The president arrived in six hundred and thirteen
Tatra 613s, with six-hundred-and-thirteen bigwigs and
then commenced a reading of six-hundred-and-thirteen
pages of a speech, which was about what six-hundred-
and-thirteen comrades had achieved and what fifteen
million more would soon achieve. Till was also up on
the platform at Windy Square. He was a Young
Pioneer with a scarf. The scarf was red and annoying,
and Till fidgeted and choked throughout the whole
speech until he couldn't bear it anymore. He untied
the scarf with the tips that formed a number one, and
because he didn't know where to put it he hung it up
on the microphone of Gustáv Husák, the president.
And because President Husák was, after the six
hundredth page of his speech, already hoarse, and
needed to clear his throat, he inadvertently reached
for the red scarf and spit his sputum into it.
"Ah, where did I stop? Yes . . ." said Gustáv Husák, the
president, smiling, as he draped the scarf back over the
microphone.
At that moment, Comrade Teacher Tomešová noticed

that Till didn't have a scarf and admonished him.
"Mind your scarf, Till," she hissed.

But as soon as Till went to reach for the scarf, Gustáv Husák was again seized by breathlessness, and beat the boy to it. When he relieved himself into the scarf again and noticed the confused Till standing between the two authorities — himself and Comrade Teacher — he apologized to the boy, in Slovak: "Sorry, kid, I didn't notice it was your Pioneer scarf."

"Never mind, Mr. President, cough into it all you want, it was choking me anyway," Till said and waved his hand.

"Ach, yes, such a smart boy," observed Gustáv Husák, the president, in the direction of the teacher.

"You know what, boy, I'll give you a chocolate bar for your scarf."

"Thank you, sir, but I'm not allowed to take chocolate from strangers!" Till objected politely.

"Tee hee, well, we have ourselves a little genius here, don't we?" Gustáv Husák said and again turned to the teacher.

"And what was his grade for morals?"

"Mr. President is no stranger," the teacher hastily explained to Till, "Mr. President belongs to us. To me, you, all the people. In our country, Till, everything belongs to everyone . . ."

"All right, I'll take hazelnut!" Till agreed.

"Hazelnut," President Husák promised, then went on
with his six-hundred-and-thirteen-page speech.
But Till never got the promised chocolate.
Some adults simply talk too much.
Especially when they get to the microphone.
Then, they're called Windbags.
Especially when they talk in Windy Square.

an appearance, elemental

On the site where the lignite mining pits are today, the old city of Brüx once stood. A poet once lived there, too. He was an erotic poet; he couldn't be otherwise. He once lived in Ústí, then in Prague. In Old Most, he searched for peace.
It was the women who drove him from place to place like the fluff of a dandelion.
But here, too, they ran him down like the elements. And so he had to sit down at the typewriter and write . . .

> *When the Labe will be above Ústí*
> *When the water begins rising*
> *I would like to fall in love*
> *With a girl from Hamburg*
> *She knows of love*
> *She knows of water*
> *Sitting at the rudder*
> *Turning and so sad*
> *I know that sadness well*
>
> *When the fire will be above Prague*
> *When Prague catches fire*
> *I would like to fall in love*

With a girl from Arc
She knows of love
She knows of fire
Gazing into the flames
Silent and so sad
I know that sadness well

When here, where I am, nothing will be
I want you to be here, at least
Mine, the most beautiful element . . .

an appearance, stony

"I hid myself in a stone, never to melt, until you, my lioness, come. You won't find me alive, merely eternal, for living is too mortal, even if, my lioness, you refuse to believe it. Stop your weeping, for your tears are nothing, if I am a lion and further, of stone.

"You won't move me . . . find another animal from the horoscope. Or Libra; Libra is just; Libra will judge which one of us is right. Whether it is I, of stone, or you, white Leo, and your dreams.

"You quivered with winter, when it was winter, and looked forward to seeing the Sun. I remember it well.

"You believed that on the Sun live small Sun People — particularly because it contradicted the astronomical theories, and all the scientific authorities conspired against you, declaring that the Sun People would burn to death.

"And you said, but what about love? Don't people burn in love? And all the scientific authorities bristled up against you, declaring that all burn up in love.

"And then you said, what about life? People don't live in life? And all the scientific authorities stood against you and said that everything living must die, but you cried.

"You were so tender-hearted, and so desperate. You

believed me and hoped I would do something with
this life, with love and also with the Sun People, that
I would tell the scientific authorities to get lost, somewhere very far away, and to spite them all and their
theories I myself would fly for the Sun People and they
would be possible, just like it's possible to live, like
love is possible . . ."

I, city, listened to the heartless things my stone lion
said and I looked everywhere for his lioness that I
might alleviate her pain from death.
But I have yet to find her.
"Here there be lions," it says on the maps of the world,
but "here there be lionesses" nowhere. Where to look
for her, then?
Fate gave me, city, only two lions.
One on the city's seal and the other on the coat of
arms at city hall.
Both are male.
And one of them is also stone.

an appearance, foolish

You will find the Liars' Bench below the large mirror opposite another large mirror on the walls of The Partisan pub.

The flower of the fibbers sits there. And there they tell tall tales, prattle, hornswoggle, narrate and spin yarns about women, and about themselves, in doing so reproducing themselves, through some sort of parthenogenesis, so that they can be with more women in many places and all at the same time, as if they'd stepped out of an infinite picture of themselves reflected in mirrors set opposite each other. I like the stories about women that come from the Liars' Bench. They never do any harm, and they all end like fairy tales.

"What's new, partners?" asks Franta Psoria, a former miner from the depths who later ran off to the carousels, lived with a Gypsy woman and got a tattoo on his left shoulder.

Those listening from the Liars' Bench know that whether it's from the pit, from the fair or from the funeral of a Gypsy baron, it will in all cases be huge, as Franta Psoria is King — King of the Liars' Bench, chosen by all.

The King smiles, takes a sip of beer, makes himself good in the mouth and talks. The men don't make a sound.

In comparison with the fables of Franta, their own lives shrink as if for microscopic observation. Franta's aware of this; he knows where his only wealth lies. He talks about the times he went down the hole as a pit foreman, and how there they had such a beautiful and full-figured bookkeeper that once, as she stood in the yard with her hands behind her back, he didn't approach her from behind to cover her eyes and ask "guess who?" like some Gymnasium student, but rather thrust his penis right into her hand. And in front of everyone she dragged him just like he was to the director, who deducted his bonuses and delivered the appropriate reprimand.

"But, gentlemen, one easily accepts the deduction of bonuses, and the reprimand along with it," Franta Psoria shouts with laughter, "when a goddess forgets to let go!"

The men laugh and slap Franta on the back. Well, some people have all the luck in the adventure of life. "A beer for the King," they order for Franta.

This is what he had: a mineshaft, youth, women, carousel, Gypsy, freedom, and a tattoo. The tattoo stayed the longest. But even this eventually left him, as had the shaft, youth, women, carousel, Gypsy, and freedom.

He got such an idiotic disease: psoriasis it's called, and it peels the skin the way it flayed his tattoo.

"Naturally," Franta Psoria turns to me, "I'm not going to tell the whole city about it!"

And he shouldn't!

He is a king only when he's a Liar.

an appearance, kosher

"A love holds me like the Jewish faith," a man with blue eyes begins his story from the Liars' Bench. "You don't believe me? Listen, then, to the story of Ráchel Šmidtová, a lawyer from the firm of Golem & Partner, of Maiselova Street in Prague. It's been many years since I studied law in Prague. More accurately, in the sixties. Well, in '68 I had to finish my studies prematurely . . . but that's another story; it has nothing to do with love.

"I was then still a shy young man, a virgin who'd never been kissed, when my classmate Ráchel Šmidtová invited me to a lecture given by Rabbi Glick at the Jewish Town Hall on Maiselova.

"Well, men, you know it from Appollinaire, don't you? It's the one with the tower with the clock whose hands go backward, because time, flying forward, is only time lost, a time that approaches death, whereas Jewish time recedes always to birth.

"But back to Miss Šmidtová . . . Something about her got under my skin, but the whole time I thought it was only the prick of the peaks of her bosom. It's only now that I realize it was her Jewish star. She got me spiritually somewhere that would take me years of climbing to reach, if I would've had to do it all on my own.

"This was accomplished by only a single lecture from Rabbi Glick. She got me there, where the body and sex begin.

"I was a bit apprehensive when I entered the lecture hall, full of white chairs. Sitting on the chairs were members of Prague's Jewish community: a wonderful people of an olive complexion, with hooked noses and dark hair. The women were so beautiful that you went cross-eyed. And the men wore their trousers with suspenders, and had on yarmulkes — as if they came from the time of Paradise, before the pogroms. They were running backward, too, just like the hands of the clock.

"I tell you, with my freckles, fair hair and blue eyes, I looked like the pope in a synagogue, but they saw me differently.

"I didn't look like them on the outside, and so they seemed to believe that my Jewishness was hidden within. And the hidden soul of a man is for the Jews more important than the crust of his skin.

"Then Rabbi Glick began. He talked about a return to the faith. He spoke in English, with such an impossible accent that I couldn't understand a word.

"Under his English words rattled something Hebrew, maybe Yiddish, maybe even Adam, the first man, before Yahweh gave him the gift of speech so he could be understood by his first wife, Lilith, which didn't quite work out.

"But my classmate Ráchel Šmidtová understood him, and from his every rattling she managed to translate the right words to Czech. She was from Adam's rib, so she understood.

" '*Zahlen Sie, bitte, Milena Jesenská, noch einmal, noch einmal*, once more, please, translate for me — my pillow to Czech,' one of Kafka's poems, written to Milenka in a letter of May 30, 1920, came to my mind. "It was in that same letter that Kafka described his loneliness.

" 'Why, when looking at strangers, am I looking at something strange? Even when I'm acquainted, nothing changes.'

"But I'm digressing, and you don't want to be kept in suspense.

"Rabbi Glick was telling a story for assimilated Jews. And that in every one of us, maybe even in Hitler, there is something assimilated, though we may have committed the most horrible atrocities. His words were taking root in my heart; green sprouts budding, leaves bursting forth, blossoms emanating from my breast.

"The story was about a young man named Aaron, who was being raised in a Tsar's cadet school in Russia, as such was the practice of the Russian Orthodox: this was the way they decimated the Jews, taking them when they were still young and re-educating them to become soldiers of the Tsar, so that they would never raise weapons for the cause of their fathers, as did Samson with the long hair.

"Aaron hadn't retained anything of his Jewish faith. He didn't observe the holidays or the Sabbath; he didn't read the Talmud or Torah; he didn't know what it meant to be a Jew.

"One day, on leave in Moscow, Aaron met the Tsar.

"He didn't know, to tell you the truth, that he was dealing with a Tsar, as the man didn't have it written on his forehead, and what's more was in disguise, as he liked to appear, to mingle with his subjects, to get to know them.

"Because it was Russia, Aaron and the Tsar began to compete in the drinking of vodka.

"Who out-drinks who and who falls under the table.

"They drank. *Nu vot!*

"They drank heroically. As the empty shots piled up, the Tsar was still ordering more. But a Tsar is a Tsar, he can buy himself a whole Lake Ladoga of vodka, a whole Baikal of the stuff, an entire Caspian Sea — Aaron ran out of cash.

"So Aaron got up, because he wasn't falling under the table just yet, and went to the innkeeper to hock his saber.

" 'Here you are,' he said to him. 'Here's a finger of our Batushka Tsar with which he shakes the world. How much vodka will it get me?'

"The innkeeper measured the saber with his eyes and said: 'For Batushka's talon, I'll give you a whole flask — let me be the loser!'

"Aaron gave a cheer, grabbed the bottle and went to the Tsar. Bum, he resolutely set the bottle down on the table. He didn't lose. He was lighter only his saber.

"But wait, gentlemen. Three days later when he had gotten over his hangover, the Tsar was stricken by a thought: what kind of an army is it that's able to squander its weapons? An army without weapons is *nichevo*, nothing!!

"The Tsar again set out for Moscow.

"He left his native Peterhof, waved goodbye to the Tsarevna and the Tsaritsa, went on his white horse Roman — the noble Romanov on the noble Roman, an English thoroughbred with a university degree in equitation.

"None of us sitting here has ever sat so high as did Nicholas, this Tsar of Romanov descent.

"Friends, that's called riding your high horse.

"Nicholas arrived at Moscow, avoiding the dive in which he'd met Aaron. He wasn't in disguise. Instead, he headed with his entourage to the barracks for an inspection.

"And believe me, it was thorough, the Tsarist inspection.

"He made the whole garrison stand in line. He cracked

his moustache like a cat-o-nine-tails, and eagle-eyed any breach of discipline in a soldier's uniform or gear, making to immediately harass the offender.

"Until he approached our Aaron. Next to Aaron stood Moshe, whose tunic was missing a button.

"He'd given it to Rebecca the day before. 'Rebecca, I know how much you like to unbutton them. Here you are, one as a keepsake,' he'd told her.

"But the Tsar had little understanding for either Moshe or Rebecca. 'Button, button, button!' he roared as other people might roar: 'Help, help, help!!' or 'Murder, murder, murderrr!!!' Well, as if a whole war would depend on a button. Tsar Nicholas, with malice in his eyes, turned to Aaron and commanded him: 'Soldier, chastise this private whose button is missing. Unsheathe your saber and stab him!'

"Yes, the absolutist emperor behaved just like this.

"None of his subjects would have had the courage to say a word. They wouldn't have had the pluck to utter their own names, to babble even a letter. They all simply shut up. Luckily, Aaron immediately recognized the Tsar as the unknown drunkard; needless to say, he knew which way the wind was blowing.

"He'd had enough presence of mind before the arrival of the inspection to have made a wooden replica of the saber, which was sheathed in his scabbard.

"To the eye it looked like a fine sword and real

enough, but he wouldn't be able to kill with it, even if he'd wanted to. Poor Moshe didn't know this; sweat trickled down his forehead. He thought he'd be killed for the sake of a stupid button.

" 'Allow me to speak, Your Majesty,' Aaron said as he clicked his heels.

" 'Speak, soldier,' Nicholas replied benevolently, with the sneer of a smile.

" 'I'll unsheathe the saber and kill, as you command, Excellency, but only if Private Moshe is truly guilty. If he is innocent, let this saber of Kuban steel transform into wood!' As he finished his speech, he unsheathed his wooden saber and poked a petrified Moshe in the chest. "Moshe stared. A miracle! The saber didn't pierce the flesh he was in the habit of nourishing, or the skin he often risked, but more often brought to Miss Rebecca, who clung to it as if she were a scented ointment.

" 'Haha, pierce me, brother, stab me, kill me, ha ha ha, I'm innocent,' Moshe screamed, then danced the saber dance around Aaron, who couldn't restrain himself and began to laugh along with him.

"Soon, the whole garrison was laughing, too.

"Even the Batushka Tsar himself was laughing.

"The horse Roman, he gave a whinny!

" 'Well, you amused me, soldier,' the Tsar said to Aaron in private. 'I forgive you the saber.'

" 'But tell me, since you're so clever — would you like

to become commander-in-chief of my army?

" 'I need skilled people. My generals have grown stupid from vodka, whores and gluttony. You with your cunning will lead my army to victory.'

"Aaron didn't waver. Should he controvert the Tsar and tempt his patience yet again?

"No, what got him off once won't get him off again.

"He accepted the Tsar's offer.

"He opted for an army career.

" 'But tell me,' the Tsar asked again, 'what an odd name you have — Aaron — it's not an Orthodox name.'

" 'No, it isn't, Your Excellency,' answered Aaron, 'it's Jewish.'

" 'A damn shame, boy, the popes christen our weapons; the highest patriarch of the Orthodox Church will bless you — you can't be a Jew and at the same time command the Tsar's army. Can you renounce your Judaism, change your name and be christened, my boy?'

" 'Yes, Your High Excellency,' answered Aaron. 'I have nothing left of my Judaism save the name given to me by my mother. I was not raised in the Jewish faith or with its customs; indeed, to be a Jew means nothing to me. There is nothing easier than to renounce something that is nothing — and actually less than nothing, because I'm at least conscious of nothing, but this I've never been conscious of. I'll be your Ivan, Batushka, your commander-in-chief of the armed forces, your Russian, your Orthodox.'

" 'That's what I call a speech, Soldier Ivan,' the Tsar rejoiced, embracing the future convert.

" 'I still have some things to take care of here, Ivan,' the Tsar informed Aaron, 'but you'll go to Petersburg with my safe-conduct. I will write to the Patriarch regarding your conversion and by the time I come to see you again, you'll be a real Russian — just like my horse Roman.

" 'Yes, he was formerly an English thoroughbred, but today? Real Romanov. Well, aren't I right?'

"The English thoroughbred gave a neigh.

"And so the carriage of the Batushka Tsar himself drove Aaron to Petersburg — originally a circumcised boy dragged into the army cadet school, a smart young man today, a future commander-in-chief of the army, which defeated even Napoleon.

" 'What's it to me, this being a Jew?' Aaron thought.

" 'Nothing, nothing, nothing at all . . . I don't know the customs of my people; I don't know what makes them suffer, what makes them laugh, what gives them consolation in their despair! I don't know the language my mother used to sing to me in. I don't know by whose hand my father perished. Did he have *payos* — was he Samson or a moneylender?

" 'O, such indifference.

" 'Where are my roots? Everything I know I learned at the cadet school of the Tsar — I've been invited to the heights by the Tsar and his God.

" 'What is Yahweh, that strict old Father, to me?

" 'In Mexico, it is said, in a desert grows a plant that doesn't have roots — where to look for sustenance in the sand, anyway? And so the plant has its roots in the air. From the air, it takes everything it needs. And the wind, which races over the sand, blows this plant without roots from place to place.

" 'This is me! A plant in Mexico.

" 'So I, chased by the wind, can drive in the carriage of the Tsar from Moscow to Petersburg, and I can transform the steel saber into wood, and I can command the corps, too — me, who yearns only for peace . . .'

"And suddenly the carriage passed over the bridge over the Volga and the God of the Jews, the God Yahweh, saw his son jumping out of the carriage, jumping over the railing of the bridge and disappearing into the wide stream.

" 'Such is a Jew. He doesn't have to know he is a Jew until someone takes from him that which is hidden. Which is what? Small but firm roots in the heart,' " Rabbi Glick finished, then looked right at me.

"I quivered. Ráchel Šmidtová translated. Then even she looked at me. It was a translated look. Actually, her look was more than that, gentlemen — hers was the look of a woman.

" 'What is hidden within?' I asked myself with caught breath.

"She revealed it. She unlocked me. She undid my buttons one after another like Rebecca from the legend. And only when I was standing before her naked did she catch sight of that that was hidden.

" 'I knew immediately you were kosher,' she told me in the morning after the night spent awake; she was gazing there, where a woman gazes at a man, 'O, rose of Sharon . . .' I looked there, too. My whole life I was ashamed. I was always different from others. My parents never told me why.

"I was ashamed before my classmates during the medical examinations, I was ashamed in the showers at the pool, I was ashamed at the army recruitment, I was ashamed while making love . . .

"And suddenly, the most beautiful woman since the time of Creation looks between my legs and says a miraculous sentence:

"I KNEW IMMEDIATELY YOU WERE KOSHER!!"

The astonished listeners on the Liars' Bench exhaled, then swallowed.

"I didn't leave her come morning. Her words were a magical *shem*. I lay back alongside her, and was as assiduous as the legendary Golem!

"And so, gentlemen, love holds me like the Jewish faith."

Overwhelmed, all the men stare with respect at this man who like his Aaron swims in a river as wide as the Volga, swimming with ardor toward a great song of life, a life that will never stop being beautiful if a magnificent Jewess tells you you're kosher. And though the men keep silent, it's a silence that's actually a fierce applause; every one in his own hidden self searches for the marvelous, the kosher, and no one protests at all when Franta Psoria, the King of the Liars, raises his hand and exclaims:

"Well, bartender, a beer's all around, on me! Come let us honor our new King!"

an appearance, human

I am a city. I'm full of people. Nothing human is
strange to me. I love people. But not because they
are great.
I love them because they are small.
There are a lot of them, and they're all lonesome.
Fettered, they yearn for freedom. They pray for
immortality, and yet they don't survive the touch of
death, the Medusa jellyfish. They thought up money
and they eternally lack it.
They explained their dreams and then they took
sleeping pills.
It's hard to survive. I, city of Most, know that — as did
Pompeii, Carthage, and ancient Rome.
O, how I know it. Just one look into the mining pit
behind the church. It's hard to survive.
It's even harder to live.
I saw a cloud in the sky yesterday.
It rode out above the city, a black conscience. This
cloud had a lance. A helmet and a shield. A horse and
rider was the cloud. Both of them skin and bone. I
knew that some of the people down there would see
them, too. People have imagination, after all.
And they will recognize that Don Quixote on his horse
can ride out of anywhere, even out of the fog, clouds

and gray smoke. Things are never explicit, are they?
At everything sad and crazy perhaps one should gaze
with imagination. Perhaps even the blackest cloud can
be transformed into a knight, tilting at windmills of
nothingness with the most virtuous of manners.
Man is insignificant and crazy.
He shouts under the arch of the bridge and exults over
the echo.
He imagines his reflection in the mirror will remain
there forever. He is conceived and he fits into his
mother's belly. He dies and fits into a small tin box.
And yet it has occurred to me that Man can be com-
pared to a cloud. Neither are what they seem to be.
Whoever has imagination can see their long lances,
the sad heights, and the most virtuous acts performed
in the name of a love.

I am a city. I'm not a tree. But I know the tree. And I
also know the wood from the tree. And the paper from
the wood of the tree I've seen innumerably.

But only a person with imagination, a man who once
stood in the mud with his head bent back observing
the dark clouds above him, could on the paper from
the wood of the tree of this world of this life on this
planet of this universe of this infinitude, write to
another person a confession of this kind:

I know I love you, even if I kid you,
And your craziness I praise to the skies,
We are the only men betrothed
You, Quixote, and me, your Cervantes.

Remember, Quixote, when once again in your armor
You ride at the mills and once again they all laugh
                                        at you,
Remember, Quixote, your author fears you,
Afraid you would stop loving him.

That you would leave him, because he didn't make
                                        you divine,
But wanted to know the whole truth of the soul.
Your author, Quixote, himself became more than
                                        ridiculous
His craziness becoming crazed — crazy through
                                        and through.

an appearance, puppy

How is it that when the children of the city are still just puppies, they prance about in my streets? How is it that when they hardly know how to walk, they already know how to run, to tear, fly about, spin, dash, sprint and scream at the apartment blocks as if they were the trees of the forest? How is it, when they should only know to fulfill their merit badges and to play their puppy-love games? They also know how to get into the orchard, whenever they want to, and how to tear apples both for their sweet taste and for the sheer joy of it all — joy, because adults lurk in the orchard. There, the grownups have already learned how to walk and forgotten how to run and have treated themselves to German shepherds; not to foster friendships with the puppies, only to frighten them, as these German shepherds keep watch over the apples and know how to tear and to bite and to run just like the puppies do, only much faster.

I am again in Vtelno, I, city, with my children, as the boys bring over the fence apples as if from the Garden of Eden. And just as in the days of the Corrida in sunny Spain when the bulls are driven out from their stalls and into the streets to undertake a frantic chase and courageously fulfill their merit badges, here the guardians of the apples hold gladiator games between the German shepherds and the puppies.

The boys escape from yellow fangs over the ugly barbed wire. The German shepherds smack the fence with their muzzles. It's a close shave. They make it by only a hair.

This time, my puppies are faster.

Breathing heavily, they bite into the Edenic fruits of childhood, seized in their frantic escape.

What's left for the German shepherds and the grownups are only the rotting apples fallen to the grass.

Thanks to their pride, they have only as much as the worms.

an appearance, final

People know they can't run away from themselves.
If they do run away, they know they'll eventually
come back.
A man takes leave of his childhood, quits babbling,
begins thinking and becomes an adult. He's reasonable, and the whole world belongs to him. Until he
begins to come back to himself. Then, he suddenly
shrinks, and when he wants to tell the people around
him that he's seen Paris, Rome and Cairo, and personally knows Sophia Loren, he finds himself beginning
to babble again, as he discovers himself coming back
to the stage of his childhood.
He hasn't gone far.
Who will be willing to listen to his babble now?
Where did he ever find comprehension? Where did
they understand him then, where will they understand
him now? Is there such a place to which he can come
back, from Paris, Rome, Cairo, from a couple of loves,
from a couple of equations among many unknowns,
from the inscrutable breast of Sophia Loren? Is there
such a place he can get to by train? Is there such a
place, where all the train conductors are poets?
Is there such a train, such a train station, whose
conductors would all recite verse to him? Is there

such a poem that can be understood by all? And what are its words?

"MOST OR BUST!" the conductors would tell him at the train station.

we, translators

Until the 15th century, in which an enormous irrigation project began, a vast swamp known as Komořanské jezero (Komoransky Lake) covered nearly the entire area of the Bohemian city of Most, in what is now the northwestern Czech Republic. A system of bridges facilitated crossing into Saxonia, the neighboring duchy of a Holy Roman Empire then just beginning the reform of its millennium-long Reich, in what is now easternmost Germany. More than metaphorically obvious, then, the Czech word *most* means — physically — "bridge."

Brüx was its name in German, an ancient form of the modern Brücke, and its earliest settlement was to become known by the name of one of its more prominent crossings, the Latinate-Slavonic Gnevin Pons, or Gneva's (Hněva's) bridge. The nearby mountain was also named after this early, and largely unknown, landlord Gneva (Gneva is a Russified spelling, Hněva its Czech corollary), and a castle later built thereupon, thus expanding the city's purview beyond its geological basin. This castle, Most's most significant settlement, was largely destroyed by its own citizens toward the end of the Thirty Years' War to prevent it from falling into the hands of the occupying Swedes. Most has a unique history of being decimated by its own citizens.

Since time immemorial, the area of and around Most has been one of the most densely populated in all of Central Europe — first settled by the Celts, then by various Germanic tribes, and in the sixth century by the Slavs, ancestors of the Czech nation. When this area was drained, Most went from being a minor provincial settlement to the largest imperial city in northwestern Bohemia, under the jurisdiction of the Přemyslids, the dynasty of the first Czech kings that ruled in Prague. One of that lineage's most notable descendants, and a passing persona in the volume at hand, was Agnes Přemyslid, daughter of the King of Bohemia; she founded the first hospital in all of Bohemia, in Prague, in addition to Most's convent of the Order of St. Clara, whose namesake (1193-1253) had been a correspondent and close friend. Before the 15th century and the discovery of brown coal, which is known as lignite — a fuel of the lowest quality that when burned produces only about half as much heat as do other, blacker, bituminous coals — tin, iron, copper and silver were mined in the vicinity as principal occupation, though inhabitants of the city also worked in light manufacture; vineyards around Hněvín were tended by the monks of the city's cloister.

Most's decline — which continues to this day — began in earnest with the Habsburgs, firstly with their rapacity for infrastructure, especially with regard to the obtainment of natural resources, and secondly with the imperial assertion of their own values, epitomized by an institutionalized oppression of Protestantism. This decline is adumbrated by the author of this book, as he has the "I" of his city speak about Blaník being "exchanged" for Bílá hora. Blaník is a mountain southeast of Prague where, according to legend, knights repose in a sort of perpetual slumber, only to rouse and ride out in a time of need to save the Czech nation from impending destruction.

Bílá hora (White Mountain) was the site of the 17th-century Habsburg victory over the Czech Estates, resulting in a renewed dark ages in which Czech culture was largely suppressed. Century-long construction began on the late-Gothic Church of the Annunciation of the Virgin Mary, Most's most notable historic landmark (here often called the "Deacon's Church"), two years after the city suffered its greatest fire in 1515. Built by the German architect Jacob Heilmann on the site of an earlier Gothic and Romanesque church, it was this structure that was famously relocated by a distance of over eight-hundred meters from its original foundations during the incredible decade-long destruction of Most, which was begun in the mid-1960s to facilitate the pursuit of the great quantity of lignite to be found beneath the Old Town. This church — foreign-built, foreign-Catholic — was one of the only buildings that survived the systematic destruction of Old Most. It was moved to stand next to Most's most venerable set of structures, creating a dismal sort of historic district: a complex of chapel and hospital, whose oldest foundations date from the 13th century, under the patronage of sv. Duch — the Holy Spirit.

At the time of the relocation of the church, many of its relics and other Baroque valuables were transferred to a small chapel in the nearby village of Vtelno, famous for the late 19th-century flowering of its apple orchards. The region between Vtelno and Most was soon filled, populated post-industrially, with an oppressive orchard of gas stations, warehouses and shopping centers that grew, and soon wilted, amid the pre-fabricated concrete apartment blocks (*paneláky*) that were the glory of communist architecture. By contrast, the attractive villas of the Zahražany quarter (the location of the area known as "Na Špačkárně" — "At the Starling House"), situated at the foot of Hněvín, were constructed at the beginning of last century. At that European *fin de siècle*, this city, too, was in its own, if modest, cultural heyday. German money financed numerous structures in the styles of the pseudo-Renaissance, Art Nouveau and Beaux Arts. These are now among the oldest surviving buildings in Most, rendering the city — architecturally, as well in many other respects — one of the "newest" cities in all of Bohemia. Moravia's Brno can boast centuries-old churches and castles. "Golden" Prague hosts its "hundred spires" and the ruins of antiquity. In contrast, and the church complex aside, Most has a handful of faded buildings dating from around the year 1900, and then mile after mile of gray concrete.

As late as 1900, the overwhelming majority of the inhabitants of Most were still of Germanic origin. However, with the extension of the train track from Ústí nad Labem to Chomutov, which served to unite Most's mines with greater Bohemia, the Czech population of the city grew steadily, eventually comprising more than one quarter of Most's inhabitants by the time of the First World War. By then, large German corporations had long appeared on the scene and had succeeded in converting the mining process from the underground "canary-in-a-cage" style to modern open-cutting, which much like quarrying requires enormous holes to be created in the surface of the earth. The owners and management were German, the machinery was German, but the workers were predominantly Czech, having come as west as their borders allowed to essentially destroy their own city in the enrichment of foreigners. It was at this time, leading up to the creation of Czechoslovakia in 1918, that Most began to be redeveloped from a so-called "boom" town of individualistic miners (think of the Yukon, or Klondike) into a major incorporated mining center. Heavy industry was its governance, and money, little of which became reinvested in Most, was its law.

In 1938, the Germans broke ground in nearby Záluží, situated between Most and Litvínov — the hometown of hockey idols Hlinka, Lang, Ručinský, Svoboda, and Šlégr — and built a chemical plant as part of the multinational Hermann Goering Werke to produce gas from the mined lignite; tens of thousands of slave laborers were worked there day and night. In 1945, nearly all the German citizens of Most were expelled under the infamous Beneš Decrees, and Czechs from all over the country began to arrive en masse, many forcibly resettled there for work purposes after 1948 by the new communist government (as referenced in this volume in "An Appearance, Manly"); they moved into the abandoned houses of Old Most, the villas in Zahražany, and the dilapidated neighboring tenements. Today, this plant manufactures oil, and pollutes the air for miles in every direction, depending on wind.

As mentioned, a plan was conceived in the 1960s to completely destroy the buildings of Old Most in order to exploit the earth underneath for its rich deposits. The idea was to level all the buildings, change the course of the Bílina riverbed (here affectionately called the Běla), and to build an enormous expanse of panel-houses around the expansion of the city ("I'm a city of reinforced concrete") in order to accommodate the majority of newly arrived citizen-workers, in the process institutionalizing oppression in the establishment of a wildly disastrous, misguidedly ultra-modern, city center. Among its many other faults, this plan greatly over-designed Most. The New Most was intended to accommodate one-hundred-thousand citizens, but Most's population at its height had been only seventy thousand. Most New or Old, much emptiness is still there. Altogether, thirty-four municipalities in the area of Most have thus far been destroyed in the pursuit of polluting, inefficient lignite — these include the pre-industrial villages such as Židovice, Libkovice, Ervěnice, Kopisty (the liquidation of this last village interrupted the ancient continuity of settlement between Most and Litvínov). And so Pavel Brycz writes in the voice of the city he's chronicling: "I am a city, a new city. I cannot bear witness to the past," for how can a city bear witness to a life predating its very existence, a life it was in many ways created to destroy? "Kde domov můj?" Brycz quotes elsewhere, "Where is my home?" — the first words of the Czech anthem, the song of a nation that for too long existed only in hope. As Brycz asks this question, so does his city. Where to find a city's home if not in itself, of itself, among its own people?

I, City — the first ever full-length English translation of Brycz's work — is many things. A collection of stories. Of prose-poems. A novel-in-stories. A series of sketches in the best easterly European tradition of Danilo Kiš, or Isaac Babel. Formal and topical inspiration can most convincingly be found in the Czech literature Brycz holds closest to his heart: the poetry of mid-century writers like Václav Hrabě and Josef Kainar (both of whom wrote texts that were to be much used as rock lyrics); Karel Konrád (1899-1971) is an essential precursor, especially in his trilogy *Robinsonáda*, *Rinaldino* and *Dinah*, a pastiche of prose and poetry that lovingly chronicles the first loves and comings-of-age of adolescent boys in Bohemia. Additionally, Karel Poláček's bucolic-humorous children's book, *Bylo nás pět* [We Were Five], is referenced here if not as a model for Brycz's work then as a model for Most's budding poets. As Brycz makes fictional people say factual things and factual people (Franz Kafka, John Paul II, the last Czechoslovak communist president Gustáv Husák) say fictional things, post-modernity via Gabriel García Márquez and other so-called Magical Realists makes its almost requisite — though noiseless — appearance.

Though Brycz's ideal is a curious sort of anthropomorphism, proposing to make his city talk, it seems the "I" purporting to be Most is much larger than anything that can be contained on a map — almost an entire consciousness, at enough of a remove from the town itself that he, she, or it can observe and can know seemingly everything, past and present. The "I" is a view not from below, which is the view of the earth, scarred beneath the city, but from above, which is the view of the transcendent, of heaven. If Brycz's "I" is to be terrestrial, though, it must be an "I" released, set free, seemingly risen from the land, which has been defiled in man's pursuit of power, to ascend high above Most's people, in order to narrate their lives, and the life of their city, from the vantage of a simpler, more hopeful future — even as the concrete panel-houses tower, too, dwarfing the spires of the Deacon's Church, in man's strained attempt at the divine.

But narration here is no straightforward affair. Brycz doesn't actually write about the people of Most, as it would seem. If pre-industrial Realism is the standard, there are no "real people" in Brycz's text; it's almost as if Brycz is implying it's impossible for "real people" to survive in Most. Rather, these mostly silent, shy and lonely beings (the Hrabalian denizens of the Liars' Bench aside) seem frozen in time, petrified, oftentimes placed in the background of any action, which is overwhelmingly historical, or an action of memory. They lose their color, fading into black and white, ghosts slowly dragging themselves on the most mundane of errands through the sooty streets. Their horror is not immediate. The one Nazi in this book does not seem particularly evil; no one in these pages gets deported to labor or re-education camps. But the horror is surely there, a cancer buried like coal. Concomitantly, Brycz never describes Most as Most, Most as a whole. Rather, his gaze lights on individual lives, on discrete histories that resist any civic coherence. Most seems like an abandoned place at the end of the world, a planet unto itself suspended in the polluted void, surrounded by "non-existence" — symbolized best in the "real world" by the Romany (Gypsy) ghetto on the outskirts of town. This area, located in the Chanov district, would be home to "the petite Gypsy woman" (if Gypsy she is), Dezider Balogh the boxer and champion urinator, and the thieves who kill and eat the dog at the villa in Zahražany, which itself is a metaphor for Most's post-communist reconstruction. Built in the 1980s especially for Most's Romany as "compensation for the unsatisfactory housing in Old Most," Chanov, a square of ruinous panel-houses, contains great poverty. It seems almost totally ungoverned even today. Public drunkenness is the norm. Unemployment is just short of total. Beyond these outskirts is *Niemandsland*, no-man's land, marked only by the Krušné hory, the Ore Mountains, over which — it is rumored — one would find Germany.

As Most's people emerge from the pollution, or from the swamp from which the town was founded, we find not individuals, despite their estrangements, despite their loneliness, but representatives. Theirs are historical lives that mistrust history, or that live it at least with typical Schweikian irony. Tellingly, many here are named Novák (which, according to the phone book, is Most's commonest surname). This is like a book about America in which almost everyone is named Smith. This abstraction, Brycz's alchemical making of archetype out of stereotype, isn't accomplished in a spirit of abuse. Brycz obviously loves his "Mosters," and has more than empathy, or sympathy — *he is one of them.* As the author, the entity most easily identified with an "I," he is their city (Most, which, as Brycz tells us, is also Prague, Paris and ancient Babylon), as are all his "Mosters," all collectively becoming the speaker and subject, experienced and experiencing only in their respective manifestations, their private existences: in what Brycz calls "appearances," which are brief revelations, or recognitions, Joycean epiphanies straight out of a Bohemian *Dubliners*. Of course, each "appearance" is modified by an adjectival subtitle. In the most ironic backwater of a cynical East, experience, like emotion, must always be qualified. In "An Appearance, Human," for example, Brycz writes, "I am a city, I am full of people. Nothing human is strange to me. I love people. And not because they are great. But because they are small, I love them." A statement naïve on the surface, but knowing underneath. Strangely for a plot of despoiled earth, nothing human is strange to it. It is talking of, and to, and maybe by, the very people who have destroyed it, who have destroyed themselves, whether they're the oldest Sudeten holdovers from before the war, or the most recent opportunists who've just come to the city to mine the last riches before the earth can give no more.

In the course of this translation, Markéta had a momentary vision of the mouth of an enormous earthmover, with the people of Most as its teeth. As it appeared to her, the machine mined the ground, despoiling the city while dulling its sharpness, its teeth — its people. The moral of this story, and of all the stories in this folk-tale-like, fairy-tale book, is that life on this planet can become a symbiotic destruction; no "I" can escape, least of all the planet itself. Recently, plans have emerged for a true "rehabilitation," one imbued with the best of the current pan-European eco-consciousness. As Most, in its conversion from geology to metropolis, has been manipulated by man ever since its inception, the prevailing idea is to relent now to nature. Unemployment is too high, the standard of living too low. Old people die, young people flee.

Most distressingly, the coal will soon all be gone. One proposal gaining support is to flood the basin beside the city, creating an enormous lake, and so returning the city to its beginnings, a primeval swamp under the mountain and its rebuilt castle — now a tourist attraction, boasting an excellent scenic overlook and a serviceable restaurant.

Prague, New York
June 2006

notes

p. 9 *Miners' strikes of Most:* Primarily wage strikes begun in response to economic crisis and widespread unemployment; 1932's was then the greatest strike in the history of labor in Central Europe.

p. 10 *Youth League shirts:* blue-colored shirts that were the uniform of adolescents (high-school age) too old to be Pioneers, too young to be allowed membership in the Communist Party.

p. 10 *Cadre profiles:* a communist-era system of personnel profiling on the basis of an individual's class background.

p. 12 *Old Town:* the original city of Most, almost completely destroyed to enable the furtherance of mining activity.

p. 14 *"Hněvín is a Mountain Magnetic":* Hněvín is situated near the Krušné hory (Ore Mountains), hence the scientific aspect of this magnetic metaphor.

p. 15 *Hradecers, Budějovicers, Brnoers or Břeclavers:* people from the Czech cities of Hradec Králové, České Budějovice, Brno, and Břeclav.

p. 17 *Laura and Her Tigers:* a popular pop-rock band founded in Most in 1985. Brycz writes texts for its successor, Zdarr.

p. 19 *Karel Poláček:* (1892–1944), Czech novelist and journalist whose most poplular book, *We Were Five*, presents life in a provincial Bohemian town through the eyes of a child.

p. 23 *August 1968:* Czechoslovakia was invaded by the armies of the Warsaw Pact on August 21, 1968, which effectively crushed the fabled "Prague Spring."

p. 24 *"Blaník had been exchanged for Bílá hora"*: Blaník is a mountain southeast of Prague. Legend has it that an army of Czech knights sleeps within only to awake to save the nation in a time of impending doom. Bílá hora (White Mountain) is now on the periphery of Prague. In 1620, it was the scene of a decisive battle in the Thirty Years' War with Holy Roman Emperor Ferdinand II routing the Czech Estates, thus ushering in centuries of Habsburg domination in Bohemia.

p. 29 *Josef Sudek:* (1896–1976), Czech photographer famous for his black-and-white landscapes; he lost his right arm in WWI.

p. 30 *Gadjo:* a derogatory term for someone not Roma.

p. 32 *"His native Haná"*: Haná is a fertile plain around Olomouc in central Moravia that was home to the Hanáks, a Slavic tribe who had their own dialect and traditions and were noted for their beautiful folk songs. Brycz uses the common female name Hanka (diminutive: Hanička) here as a metaphor for the region and its people.

p. 33 *Where is My Home:* "Kde domov můj?," the Czech national anthem.

p. 33 *"Like those from Letohrádek"*: Letohrádek Hvězda in Prague was built by Archduke Ferdinand of Tyrol in the mid-16th century as a star-shaped summer/hunting seat. Legend claims that during the Battle of White Mountain the brave Moravians defended its walls to the last man. Many historians claim that the Moravians were actually fleeing back to Prague and became trapped at the walls and were left with no other option but to fight.

p. 35 *"Up to Paradise"*: Český ráj (Czech Paradise), a national nature preserve east of Most.

p. 35 *Ginger:* the city of Pardubice is famous for their gingerbread cakes; "gingerbread" is also slang for pervitin, the notorious Czech-made methamphetamine, first introduced by the Nazis for their soldiers at the front.

p. 42 *Svinčice:* a village ten kilometers from Most known for its horse breeding and stables.

p. 44 *"Sinful people are not only to be found in the city of Prague":* a reference to the TV crime serial *Hříšní lidé města pražského* [Sinners of Prague] in which a band of detectives valiantly fights the city's underworld. The show debuted in 1968 and ran for a number of years.

p. 44 *Buzuluk:* a town in the Orenburg province of Russia and the site of a three-day-long battle in June 1918 between units of the Czechoslovak Legion and the Bolsheviks. During WWII, the 1st Czechoslovak Independent Field Brigade was formed there. Commanded by future president Ludvík Svoboda, it fought alongside the Red Army.

p. 45 *Dalibor:* a 15th-century legend best known through its 1868 retelling as a story of revenge in Bedřich Smetana's opera. Dalibor is said to have been a knight who led a rebellion of Czech serfs against a fellow knight, Adam of Drahonice. Prior to his execution as punishment for this betrayal of his class, Dalibor was imprisoned in a tower at Prague Castle, now known as Dalibor Tower.

p. 50 *Winnetou: Last of the Renegades:* one of a series of German-language Westerns shot in the 1960s in Yugoslavia and based on the writings of Karl May (1842-1912). The films, immensely popular in Eastern Europe in the 1960s and 1970s, had the Indian Winnetou (Pierre Brice) and Old Shatterhand (Lex Barker), his sympathetic white friend of Germanic descent, join forces to fight against white settlement, which in these movies often represents capitalism and its threat to the nativist "Red Man."

p. 56 *"A chemical plant established by Hitler"*: built in nearby Záluží, part of the Hermann Goering Werke.

p. 57 *Blues Bouillon:* a local band and a reference to the tradition of giving out goulash at campaign rallies.

p. 60 *"Could be that war in the bay"*: the Yugoslav Wars of the 1990s.

p. 68 *"Without the firing of a single shot"*: referring to the relatively peaceful dissolution of communism in Eastern Europe, particularly Czechsolovakia's Velvet Revolution in 1989.

p. 68 *Vlastimil Harapes:* Czech dancer, choreographer, and actor, born 1946.

p. 71 *Winterhilfe:* literally "Winter-help," the Winter Relief Program of the Nazi Party, founded in order to support its members during the Great Depression of 1932.

p. 78 *Švanda the bagpiper:* a musician who makes a Faustian bargain to free himself for the woman he loves. In its operatic treatment by Czech composer Jaromír Weinberger (1896-1967), Švanda's bagpipes compel one to dance.

p. 85 *Agnes Přemyslid:* (1211-1282), daughter of the King of Bohemia, a woman of religion and charity, and, in 1989, the first Eastern Bloc saint to be canonized by Pope John Paul II.

p. 91 *Jizerská 50:* a 50k cross-country ski race held yearly in the Jizerské Mountains of north Bohemia.

p. 108 *Gustáv Husák:* (1919-1991), leader of the Communist Party of Czechoslovakia during the period of Normalization in the 1970s and '80s, president from 1975 to 1989. As a Slovak, he famously had trouble speaking Czech fluently, despite the close similarities between the languages.

p. 108 *Tatra 613:* the T613 was a Czech car manufactured in the 1970s. Tatra was the largest car-maker in Czechoslovakia, and after Daimler Mercedes-Benz and Peugeot, is the oldest still-functioning vehicle manufacturer in the world.

p. 108 *Windy Square:* not an official square in Most, but perhaps named after the "longwindedness" of President Husák and his ilk.

p. 111 *"When the Labe will be above Ústí":* an impossibility as Ústí nad Labem, a large industrial city in north Bohemia, means literally Ústí above the Labe (Elbe).

p. 118 *Maiselova Street:* the main street of Josefov, the former Jewish Ghetto of Prague, named after its most famous mayor, Mordechai Maisel (1528-1601).

p. 118 *"Jewish time recedes always to birth":* a reference to the clock on the tower of the Jewish Town Hall on Maiselova Street. As the clock's hours are represented by letters of the Hebrew alphabet, which is read from right to left, its hands run counterclockwise.

p. 120 *"Kafka described his loneliness":* referring to Kafka's love affair, only partially epistolary, with his Czech translator, Milena Jesenská (1896-1944).

p. 121 *Nu vot!:* a Russian exclamation, meaning roughly "Now what!" or "And so!"

Pavel Brycz was born in 1968 in Roudnice nad Labem and grew up in Most. After receiving a degree in Czech language from the Pedagogical Faculty of Ústí nad Labem, he moved to Prague to study at the drama academy (DAMU), taking a degree in dramaturgy in 1994. Later employed as a copy-writer for an advertising agency, perhaps his best known "work," though he has never been widely credited for it, is the slogan he wrote for the Czech Kentucky Fried Chicken franchise: "damn good chicken." At present he resides in Jablonec nad Nisou with his wife and three sons, teaches Czech language and literature at a Gymnasium in Liberec, hosts a program for children on Czech Radio, and writes texts for the Balkan-chanson-jazz-folk band Zdarr.

I, City is Brycz's third book, and for it he was awarded the Jiří Orten Prize, given yearly to the best work by an author under the age of thirty. He has written two novels and two story collections since. His novel *Sloni mlčí* [2002; Silent Elephants] was written in France while on a UNESCO stipend, and his latest novel, *Patriarchátu dávno zašlá sláva* [2003; The Waning Fame of Our Forefathers], won him the Czech State Prize for Literature in 2004, its youngest recipient ever. In English his work has appeared in *Daylight in Nightclub Inferno* (Catbird Press, 1997) and in a number of magazines.

about the translators

JOSHUA COHEN is the author of *The Quorum* (Twisted Spoon Press, 2005). A co-editor of *Blatt*, his fiction has appeared in numerous publications and anthologies, and his essays appear regularly in the *Forward*. He lives in Brooklyn, New York.

MARKÉTA HOFMEISTEROVÁ was born and lives in Prague. After studying at Charles University, she began contributing essays to various literary publications and has translated into Czech two volumes of the collected stories of Leonard Michaels.

I, CITY

by Pavel Brycz

Translated by Joshua Cohen & Markéta Hofmeisterová
from the Czech original *Jsem město* (Most: Hněvín, 1998)

Design by J. Slast
Set in Univers Condensed / Janson
Cover and end-leaf images come from
Most 1932-1982 (Most: Městský národní výbor, 1982)

This is a first edition published in 2006 by
TWISTED SPOON PRESS
P.O. Box 21 – Preslova 12
150 21 Prague 5, Czech Republic
info@twistedspoon.com / www.twistedspoon.com

Earlier versions first appeared in:
Absinthe: New European Writing
Prague Literary Review

Distributed by
SCB DISTRIBUTORS
15608 South New Century Drive
Gardena CA, 90248
toll free: 1-800-729-6423
info@scbdistributors.com / www.scbdistributors.com

Printed and bound in the Czech Republic
by PB Tisk